SQUADRON
SCRAMBLE

SQUADRON SCRAMBLE

Yeoman in the Battle of Britain

Robert Jackson

Walker and Company
New York

Oz Edition

First published in the United States of America
in 1985 by the Walker Publishing Company, Inc.

Library of Congress Cataloging in Publication Data

Jackson, Robert, 1941–
  Squadron scramble.

  1. World War, 1939–1945—Fiction. 2. Britain, Battle
of, 1940—Fiction. I. Title.
PR6060.A26S6   1985   823'.914   84-27050
ISBN: 0-8027-0839-0

Printed in the United States of America

10 9 8 7 6 5 4 3 2 1

Chapter One

IT WAS DAWN, AND THE REFLECTED RAYS OF THE morning sun formed a golden avenue over the surface of the sea. They touched the castle of Lindisfarne and the ruined pinnacles of the monastery beyond it, and in them the seabirds wheeled like snowflakes, screaming as hunger drove them towards the offshore feeding grounds.

Here, on this rugged outcrop jutting out from the Northumbrian coast, many pages of Britain's early history had been written. Two thousand years ago, this had been the land of the Celtic tribe of the Votadini; they had survived until the coming of the Sea Wolves, the Anglo-Saxon raiders who had smashed the British kingdoms in the north, vestiges of the fallen Roman Empire, and established their own kingdom of Bernicia.

It was here, a century later, that Christianity had first taken root in northern Britain, sown by the followers of Columba of Iona. They had endured, weathering the storms of nature and man, stolidly rebuilding what later sea-raiders were to destroy. Wars and skirmishes came and went, breaking on the ageless rocks of Lindisfarne like the sea itself.

The bells of the monastery were silent now, only the ruined stones retaining the memory of their echoes, and the seas that lashed the iron-bound cliffs of the Northumbrian coast brought with them a greater menace than Britain had ever known. Signs of that menace came with the tide in a hundred different ways. Empty crates, some of them seared by fire; oil from ruptured fuel tanks;

articles of clothing and pathetic personal belongings; and sometimes, a lifejacket or an empty, overturned lifeboat.

A man sat on the castle mound, his back against the weathered stones, and gazed out across the sea. Once, he had gleaned a meagre living from combing the beaches to the south; but now the beaches were denied to him, sown with mines and barbed wire, and he had little to do with his life but gaze out over the water that had once been father and mother to him. He managed to exist; odd jobs brought in a few shillings, and he received a small pension because he had lost a leg at Jutland.

He was old, but his eyes were still keen, and he narrowed them against the wind as a speck came into view, moving low over the horizon from north to south. He watched it without much interest. It came almost every day, usually at the same time, and he knew it was an enemy aircraft; but it stayed well clear of the coast, brought no harm to Lindisfarne, and went on its way unmolested.

The old man removed his pipe and spat. They had a cushy job, those airmen. He thought of his own son, still in hospital suffering from severe burns and the after-effects of exposure after clinging to a raft for two days when the aircraft carrier HMS *Glorious* was sunk off Norway. The old seaman raised a hand and wiped away a sudden tear. What was a twenty-four-year-old going to make of his life, with half his face missing?

Three miles out over the sea, the pilot of the Dornier 18 flying-boat watched the sunrise lighting up the Northumbrian coastline. He was a year younger than the old man's son, yet already he was one of the most experienced operational pilots of Maritime Reconnaissance Group 31. Over the past eight months, operating from the group's base in Heligoland, he and his crew had ranged as far afield as Norway's North Cape, shadowing the movements of the British Home Fleet.

It had not all been easy. The group had lost four crews

during the Norwegian Campaign, one of them shot down by, of all things, an elderly Avro Anson of RAF Coastal Command. The gunner had survived to tell the tale.

The group's task now, during these first days of August 1940, was to plot the movements of British coastal convoys and pass on the information to Luftwaffe Intelligence. The Battle of France had ended six weeks earlier, and now the Luftwaffe was gathering its strength for an all-out onslaught against England. Already, the German bombers had been pounding the convoys in the Channel with the primary aim of bringing the British fighter squadrons into action; but the British had been clever, carefully husbanding their reserves of Spitfires and Hurricanes for the main battle that was to come, instead of frittering them away in skirmishes.

Today, the North Sea was empty. There was no sign of any shipping, creeping southwards in the shelter of the coast; just a few fishing craft that were not worth bothering about. Another five minutes, and it would be time to turn for home.

Had the Dornier pilot but known it, his presence had not gone undetected. Off Eyemouth, naval personnel on board an innocent-looking trawler had already flashed details of the German aircraft's course and speed to a communications centre at Rosyth. From there, the information had been transmitted to the RAF Fighter Control Room at Ouston, in Northumberland. A flight of Hurricanes from Acklington had searched for the Dornier, but failed to locate it; the grey-camouflaged aircraft was difficult to spot, flying low above the waves.

The young Dornier pilot had just begun to turn away from the coast, his mission completed, when his gunner gave a shout of alarm over the intercom. The pilot tightened the turn, looking back as he did so, and in that instant he saw the British fighter.

It was a Spitfire, flying so low that its slipstream furrowed the sea. The Dornier's gunner opened fire and the pilot saw an avenue of white splashes creep towards the British fighter. Then the Spitfire opened up too, and suddenly the interior of the Dornier's fuselage was a nightmare of flying metal and screaming men as a solid burst of machine-gun fire tore into it. The rear gun ceased firing abruptly. The navigator shrieked, rose from his seat and took a few stumbling steps aft, both hands clasped over his eyes. He was already dead; a bullet had removed the top of his skull. He fell in a heap and lay still.

The Spitfire came in again, this time from the beam, firing as the Dornier turned away desperately. The young pilot screamed as a bullet shattered his right shoulder blade and emerged just under the collar bone, a white-hot lance of agony. He coughed, and blood spattered the front of his flying overall.

Somehow, he retained control, pointing the bow of the flying-boat out to sea. He managed to twist in his seat and look back through a red mist of pain, in time to see the Spitfire curving in for another attack. A devout Roman Catholic, he closed his eyes for an instant and forced his numbed brain to make an act of contrition. Then he waited for the burst of fire that would send the Dornier and its crew to their graves.

It never came. Instead, the Spitfire swept past, climbed and turned, and came in from astern once more. There was still no fire, and the British pilot repeated the procedure all over again. He pursued the crippled flying-boat for another couple of minutes, then turned and flew away towards the land.

The Dornier limped out to sea. It was riddled with holes, but both engines were still running. The pilot, coughing up his lungs and passing out from time to time with pain, somehow managed to hold his course. Each time he fainted, he pulled the flying-boat's nose up just in time to avoid diving into the water.

Ninety minutes later, he saw a ship. It was a German minesweeper. At his last gasp, he smacked the Dornier down on to the sea a hundred yards from the vessel. A boat put out, and seamen lifted him from the shattered cockpit, together with the bodies of the rest of the crew. On the captain's orders, gunners sank the flying-boat with two rounds.

The pilot lingered in delirium for two days before he died. They buried him at sea. A month later, his mother received a letter of sympathy, bearing the Führer's signature in facsimile. She tore it up and threw it on the fire.

Yeoman lay on the hillside, his head pillowed on his tunic, his eyes fixed on a sparrowhawk. He had been watching the bird for the past ten minutes, following its movements as it quartered the ridge on the other side of the river. He marvelled at the methodical way in which it sought out its prey, dividing the ridge into fifty-yard sections and then hovering, its keen eyes sweeping the undergrowth. If only we had eyes like that, he thought, the Huns wouldn't stand a chance.

He stretched, luxuriating in the evening sunshine. It had been a murderously hot day, but now a light breeze blew up the Swale valley, bringing with it a welcome coolness. Yeoman loved this spot. Below him, the river rippled between wooded banks, curving away along the outskirts of Richmond, Swaledale's ancient capital, dominated by the square, solid keep of its Norman castle. On his left, hidden behind the trees, lay the ruined abbey of Easby, among whose stones he had surreptitiously searched for jackdaws' eggs as a child.

He had waited a long time for this short spell of leave. It was just a pity, he reflected, that he had not been able to celebrate his last operational patrol with a victory; he would have got that Dornier recce kite for certain, if his wretched guns hadn't jammed at the crucial moment. Anyway, he had managed to put a few bursts into the flying-boat before it disappeared out to sea, so perhaps it hadn't made it home after all.

9

He lay there, recalling his hectic three weeks in France. It all seemed a long time ago, but in fact it was only two and a half months since he had made his escape from Dunkirk with the battered, bloodied men of the British Expeditionary Force. The memory of it seemed unreal now, as did that of his six victories. If ever I go back to journalism after all this is over, he wondered, and write about what I have experienced, the people I have known, will my memory paint an accurate picture, or will it all be blurred and distorted by the passage of time?

One memory at least was clear, and in remembering he felt a sudden upsurge of warmth. Julia. Julia Connors, the lovely, red-haired American war correspondent with whose help he had escaped from under the very noses of the Germans after being shot down. They had parted in Paris, and although he had contacted the London office of her newspaper several times since his return to England, there had been no news of her.

Then, quite out of the blue, he had received a letter. It had reached him via his squadron. He sat up and drew it carefully from the breast pocket of his tunic, smoothing it out and re-reading it for the hundredth time. The handwriting was small and neat, and sloped backwards. Yeoman smiled to himself; so Julia was left-handed. He hadn't noticed before.

Dear George,
I hope this is going to get to you sooner or later. I have to know how you are, and what's become of you. It was three weeks before I got out of France after I left you, but that's a long story. The main thing is that I'm OK, and I'm praying you are too.

I don't know where you are, George, or even if you'll ever read this. But if you do, and are able to, please drop me a line. I would very much like to hear from you again. Maybe we can get together, if you are in the London area. I'd love to see you. Till then, look after yourself. Don't get up to anything too rash.

Love, Julia.

He sighed and folded the letter away again. He had given up trying to read between the lines. Perhaps she was just taking a genuinely friendly interest in his welfare; on the other hand, it might be something more. He could only hope. The trouble was that he had a kind of inferiority complex where Julia was concerned; he couldn't imagine that she would be seriously interested in a mere sergeant pilot, that she might want their relationship, founded on so short an acquaintance, to develop into something deeper than friendship.

Julia had occupied his mind more than he cared to admit over the past few weeks. Anyway, he told himself, there was little point in further speculation over her possible feelings towards him. He had replied to her letter, and if she still wished it he would see her as soon as he could. In the meantime, he would try to put the distracting image of her out of his mind.

Suddenly, he wanted to be back in action again. There had been a time, just after his return home, when he had never wanted to hear the sound of gunfire again; but after a period of rest he, like most of the other fighter pilots he knew, was once more itching for a crack at the enemy.

A lot had happened during the past two months. Immediately after Dunkirk Yeoman's squadron, Number 505, had moved to Leconfield in Yorkshire, where it had exchanged its tired Hurricanes for Spitfires. Under the merciless drive of their co, Hillier, newly promoted to the rank of wing commander, the pilots had trained hard, mastering their new fighters.

Yeoman had taken to the Spitfire almost at once, finding the nimble fighter a sheer delight to fly, but some of his colleagues had grumbled that they would have preferred to keep their Hurricanes. He grinned as he remembered the plight of his friend, Jim Callender, the 'Tiger from Texas' who boasted an American father and an English mother. Callender had decided, in the middle of a solo aerobatic session over the Yorkshire coast, to beat up Scarborough. Coming out of a loop, he had pushed the stick forward rather abruptly to send the Spit into a dive. He might have got away with it in a Hurricane, but the Spitfire hated rough treatment of this kind.

Several things had happened in rapid succession, all of them catastrophic and all of them elaborated on at length by Callender when he came to tell the story in the mess. First of all, his engine had stopped dead. Then a stream of fuel had shot out of the vent pipe in front of the windshield and splashed all over the cockpit canopy. In the split second it took for this to happen, Callender had been lifted bodily out of his seat to the full extent of his safety belt, accompanied by a shower of dust and bits of paper from the bottom of the cockpit. By the time his backside connected with his seat again the Spit was going down in a vertical dive, its propeller windmilling. The pilot had closed the throttle, then opened it again cautiously; to his relief the engine responded and he brought the Spit out of its headlong plunge with barely five hundred feet to spare, howling over the rooftops of Scarborough like a tornado.

The carburettor had been the trouble. Experienced Spitfire pilots were in the habit of losing height quickly by rolling the Spit over on its back and pulling back the stick, which did not interrupt the fuel flow. Callender had learned the hard way.

In July the squadron had moved up to Usworth, near Sunderland, which it shared with the Hurricanes of 607 Squadron. Together with other fighter units on the north-east coast, its task was to intercept German reconnaissance aircraft and the occasional bomber that ventured into the area. Yeoman had found the job dull, never sighting an enemy machine until his encounter with the Dornier 18 the day before he went on leave. Still, he was sure that the squadron would be moving south fairly soon; the fighter squadrons in the south-east had already seen considerable action over the Channel, and some of them must be due for a rest. In that case, their place would be taken by the squadrons now in the north, in Number 13 Group's area.

The sun was well down now, partly hidden by the trees, and the breeze was growing chilly. Yeoman got up and put on his tunic, brushing bits of grass from it and tugging to straighten out the creases. He had lost all his kit in France and the tunic was new – as new as the ribbon of the Distinguished Flying Medal that gleamed proudly on his breast. He still felt self-conscious when he thought about the medal; there were others, he thought, who had deserved the award far more than himself. Nevertheless, the ribbon told the world that its wearer was not a new boy any more, that he had achieved something.

He walked down the steep incline that fell away through the trees, vaulting a low wall on to a rocky path that eventually joined the Richmond–Catterick road. He retrieved his push-bike from its resting place among a bed of nettles, where he had carelessly dropped it, and bumped his way along the path, wobbling round the biggest of the stones.

He reached the road and turned right, panting up the hill past St Mary's Church and the old grammar school – closed now for the summer holidays – where he had spent much of his boyhood, and turned left into the market place. The clock on Trinity Church showed five to eight, and for a summer's evening there were curiously few people about. A small group of soldiers on a street corner broke off their earnest conversation with some local girls to throw catcalls after him as he cycled past, but he took no notice.

He had arranged to meet his father, John Yeoman, at an old pub called the Black Bull, up a winding street on the other side of the market place. His father lived in a small village a couple of miles out of Richmond, but one evening in the local there had been enough for both of them. George had become something of a hero, discovering to his surprise that there had been a write-up about him in the local evening paper, and although both he and his father were secretly proud of the fact, the constant back-slapping and beer-buying had soon become an embarrassment. At least in town they could enjoy a drink and a game of darts in peace.

He dismounted outside the Black Bull and wheeled his cycle through to the back yard, pushing it out of sight behind some beer barrels. These were times when no personal property was safe, especially near an army camp the size of Catterick, and a bicycle would be fair game for any soldier who happened to miss the last bus back to barracks.

John Yeoman was already in the bar, halfway through his second pint and contemplating the smoke curling upward from his favourite cherrywood pipe, when his son walked in. The two nodded to each other. There was little outward sign of affection, but in fact they shared a deep mutual respect and admiration. Since the death of George's mother in the influenza epidemic of 1919, when George was only a baby, John had brought up the boy single-handed, and no one would deny that he had done a good job of it. John was a gamekeeper, and much respected in the neighbourhood; it was his eternal pride that the respect extended to his son, and now that George was back from France, with a decoration into the bargain, his cup was full.

The landlord, a chubby man with a round, red face and white hair brushed straight back, grinned at Yeoman and pushed a pint across the bar. He winked.

'That's on the house, and it's the real stuff, too – none of that watered-down rubbish you'll get in some places, I can tell you.' He leaned over the bar. 'Your old feller here's been telling me a bit about you. I reckon you've earned that pint, and a few more. I was a rigger with the

14

RFC in Belgium during the last lot, so I know a bit about it all.'

Yeoman smiled, thinking: no you don't. You don't know about Panzers racing across the countryside so fast that nothing can stand in their way; you've never heard the screech of Stukas, coming down smack between your eyes. I hope to God we can prevent it happening here.

He looked reproachfully at his father, who coughed and looked away. Yeoman dug him playfully in the ribs. 'Come on, you old gossip,' he said, 'I'll give you a hammering at darts.' The landlord laughed. 'That'll be the day. Throws a fair arrow, does John.' He rubbed a finger along the side of his nose. 'He's pretty handy with a twelve-bore, too. We've had a few pheasants between us, I can tell you.'

'Shut up, Frank. You'll cost me my job one of these days, with that great mouth of yours.'

John Yeoman turned to the dartboard and threw three darts in rapid succession. They stuck in double twenty, treble twenty and bull. His son inspected the board in mock awe. 'Bloody hell!' he commented.

His father glared at him. 'Since when did you start swearing?' he asked.

'When I crashed my first Hurricane,' Yeoman grinned. Frank, the landlord, polished the counter with a flourish. 'Get your arse smacked for that sort of thing,' he grunted.

The darts game went on, with banter flying back and forth across the bar. In the end, with his father four games up, Yeoman threw down his darts in disgust. 'All right,' he said, 'that's about eight pints I owe you. You might as well make a start on them.'

They pushed their way back to the bar. The pub had started to fill up, and Yeoman looked round with interest. His was the only RAF uniform in the place; the rest were khaki. At a table near the wall, four or five soldiers were conversing loudly in a strange language. Yeoman saw the 'Poland' flash on their shoulders.

There was a sudden commotion and the door into the bar was flung wide open. The background buzz of conversation died away and heads turned in curiosity as three soldiers barged their way into the room, two of them partly supporting the third. They looked around them, and one of them said: 'Oh, come on, this place is as dead as a doornail. Let's go somewhere else.'

The man in the middle suddenly jerked his arms, throwing off his companions' hands, and stood swaying in the doorway. Yeoman saw that the man was not merely drunk; he appeared to be in an advanced state of nerves and was trembling violently. He fixed a glassy eye on the pilot and took a few unsteady steps towards him, his lips bared in something like a snarl.

'Brylcreem bastard!' he hissed. 'Where were you? Where was the bastard Air Force at Dunkirk?'

One of his friends stepped forward and took him by the elbow. 'Oh, for God's sake leave it,' he said. 'Let's just get out of here.'

The soldier came closer to Yeoman, his breath reeking of drink. 'Where were you?' he repeated. 'Where were you when we were having the shit bombed out of us?'

His friend made an apologetic gesture. 'Sorry about this, mate,' he said. 'He had a hell of a rough time. Saw a lot of his pals go down.'

Yeoman nodded, conscious of a silence so heavy that it might have been cut with a knife. 'I know how he feels,' he said calmly. 'I was there myself.'

The apologetic soldier looked taken aback. The pilot's words, however, failed to make any impression on his drunken companion. He tore his arm savagely away from the other's restraining grasp and took a sudden swing at Yeoman's face. It missed its target, but caught the pilot a painful blow on the shoulder. He staggered off to one side and his assailant fell against the bar, striking his head.

Yeoman recovered his balance and prepared to meet another assault. It was not necessary. The soldier was lying senseless on the floor. One of his companions knelt beside him and the other started to apologize again, but Yeoman waved him to silence. The pilot nodded to the landlord and walked out of the bar, followed by his father.

Outside, he leaned against a wall in the darkness, breathing deeply. He felt upset and physically sick. The drunken soldier's name was Ken Harrison. He had been one of Yeoman's best friends at school.

Chapter Two

A HEAVY BLANKET OF CLOUD HUNG LOW OVER ABBE-ville airfield. Tendrils of fog crept in from the Channel, partly shrouding the angular lines of the Messerschmitts which were dispersed around the airfield's perimeter.

In the briefing room, the pilots of Fighter Wing 66 looked at one another through the curling blue streamers of cigarette smoke. They wondered what was going on. They had only just arrived at Abbeville after a period of rest and re-equipment following substantial losses in the Battle of France a few weeks earlier, and now they were eager to come to grips with the RAF.

One of the wing's youngest pilots, Lieutenant Joachim Richter – already a flight commander with Number Three Squadron, in spite of his youth – glanced out of the window. The fog seemed to be getting worse; it didn't look at all promising.

The pilots suddenly sprang to attention with a clatter of chairs as the commander of Fighter Wing 66, Colonel Becker, strode into the room and mounted the dais at the far end, followed by a small comet's tail of officers. He motioned to them to sit down. A deep silence fell as he spoke.

'Today, gentlemen, is one you will remember. Today, 13 August 1940, is Eagle Day – the start of our great air offensive against England.'

A hubbub of conversation broke out, with all the pilots talking at once. Becker held up his hand for silence.

'As you are aware,' he continued, 'our bombers have

been attacking British convoys in the Channel for a month now. We had hoped to bring up the RAF in strength so that our own fighters could inflict losses on it before the start of our main offensive. Unfortunately the RAF refused to co-operate. So we can expect a fair amount of opposition.'

Richter exchanged looks with his neighbour, Franz Peters. Their thoughts were unspoken, but clear nevertheless. Both had fought the RAF during the Battle of France, and knew what tough fighters the British could be. Now, with the Tommies fighting for their very homeland, there would be no quarter. They turned their attention back to Becker.

The latter made a signal to the wing's Intelligence officer, who pulled a cord. A blind shot up, revealing a large map of southern England. There were a lot of circles on it, in various colours.

'Yesterday,' Becker went on, 'a special Luftwaffe unit operating out of Calais-Marck with Messerschmitts adapted to carry bombs – a preposterous idea, but one which in fact worked extremely well – attacked a series of British radio-location stations here on the south-east coast.'

He tapped the map with a long pointer.

'These stations are, if you like, the "eyes" of the British radio-location network, by which means they can locate our bombers while they are still some distance away. We believe that as a result of this attack, and others later in the day, at least half the stations are now out of action. This, at least, should give our bombers a fighting chance of getting through.

'The destruction of these stations was the preliminary aim of Operation "Eagle Attack". Now the second phase can begin.' He paused and surveyed the assembled pilots.

'Today, at 14.00 hours, Luftflotten Two and Three will launch a maximum-effort attack against RAF airfields in south-east England. Their object will be to disrupt the

RAF's ground organization and to bring the British fighters to combat. Our bombers will, of course, have a strong fighter escort. We shall not be part of it.'

A murmur of disappointment rippled round the briefing room. Becker held up his hand once more and grinned.

'Don't worry, gentlemen,' he went on, 'there will be plenty for us to do. Our job will begin when our bombers are returning to base and the Tommies are on the ground, refuelling and rearming. We are to go in and hit them on their airfields – hard!'

Becker thumped the pointer on the dais and stood with his legs apart, holding it like a grounded spear, surveying the pilots with an almost theatrical air. Abruptly, he turned to the wall map and indicated three red circles.

'Here are the details. Major Meurer's Number One Squadron will attack Hawkinge, here. Major Runge's Number Two Squadron will go for Lympne, here, and Number Three Squadron under Major Hartwig will strike at Manston.' The pilots, heads bent, scribbled bits of information on cigarette packets or the backs of their hands as Becker continued to pour out information in a staccato stream.

'Take off will be at 15.00 hours. We shall form up as a wing over Abbeville and fly to Point Friedrich, here – ' he tapped a square on the map in mid-Channel – 'when Number Three Squadron will break away on my orders to attack its objective. Numbers One and Two Squadrons will then turn on to 225 degrees and fly parallel to the coast. Again on my instructions, these two squadrons will split up and head for their own targets.

'On the outward trip, we shall maintain an altitude of not more than one hundred feet. At that height, it won't be easy for the Tommies to pick us up. Immediately on breaking off, each squadron will climb like hell to ten thousand feet, followed by a steep dive on to their targets. In this way we ought to be able to get in, make two or three firing passes, and get out again without too much trouble from the flak.

'Everything depends on accurate timing. We have got to catch the Tommies with their pants down and dish out as much punishment as we can. If we don't, our bombers are likely to suffer.'

The briefing continued, the pilots making notes of radio frequencies, emergency procedures, navigational details and weather conditions. Afterwards, they converged on their respective messes for breakfast.

Richter and Peters sat over their coffee, discussing the forthcoming mission. The weather was still poor, but according to the met. men it would start to clear about noon. Peters leaned back in his chair and looked at his companion.

'I just hope the Tommies are as dense as Luftwaffe High Command think they are,' he said. 'Somehow, I can't imagine that they would put all their fighters into the air at once and then have 'em all on the ground at the same time. I also think they might have a few more Spitfires and Hurricanes up their sleeve than our Intelligence people believe. After all, they didn't throw too many away in the French campaign, or on convoy protection, as we hoped they would.'

Richter nodded thoughtfully. 'I think we'll be pretty evenly matched in terms of numbers. It's tactics that will give us the edge. The Tommies were still using their tight battle formations when we last met them, and I don't suppose anything has changed since then. No, what bothers me is that bloody Channel. We both know that the Emil flies like a brick with battle damage, and that long drag over the sea is going to be the downfall of a few of us.'

He paused, recalling his own bitter experience of the English Channel; his escape from a burning Messerschmitt, his capture by British troops in the Dunkirk perimeter. He had got away by the skin of his teeth, when the boat that was taking him out to a British ship overturned during an air attack; he had clung to the post of a jetty for two days, with troops tramping overhead, before German soldiers finally discovered him, more dead than alive. It was an experience he did not wish to repeat.

He lowered his voice. 'Franz,' he continued, 'I'm not joking. I think if I'm badly hit, I would rather bale out over Tommyland than risk ditching in the Channel. I've had my fill of salt water.'

The other laughed. 'I've had my fill of any kind of water. Fishes fornicate in it. This stuff's more in my line, you bloody old pessimist.' He pulled out the hip-flask he always carried and poured a small measure into a fresh cup of coffee. Outside, mechanics were running-up the engines of their Messerschmitts. There was nothing to do now but wait.

Fifteen hundred hours. The fog had dispersed now and the clouds had broken up. The strong afternoon sun shone on the blotchy camouflage of the wing's forty Messerschmitt 109s as they taxied out for take off. They thundered down Abbeville's runway in fours and formed up overhead.

On the other side of the Channel, a radar operator saw a faint 'blip' shimmer briefly on his screen over the French coast. Before he could take a bearing on it, it disappeared. He shrugged and picked up the mug of tea which a pretty young WAAF placed beside him.

The Messerschmitts roared over the coast and dropped down to a hundred feet, the glittering sea a blue-grey blur beneath them. The whole formation set course 358 degrees, heading north.

Slightly ahead of the formation, Colonel Becker glanced at his chronometer. Point Friedrich coming up in fifteen seconds. Ushant was behind them and Calais over on the left.

Becker rocked his wings. As though tied together, the

fifteen Messerschmitts of Number Three Squadron bounded skywards, clawing for altitude. The rest of the formation turned through a half-circle, the wingtips of the lower aircraft almost brushing the sea, and followed the English coastline for some distance. Then they, too, began climbing hard.

The three flights of Number Three Squadron climbed in line astern. Richter, leading Number Two Flight, peered through the light haze at the coast to get his bearings. There was Dover, easily recognizable, with Deal coming up under the nose. Beyond it, sprawled on its headland, was Ramsgate. Richter let his eyes travel to the left of the town, following the pencil-line of the Ramsgate–Canterbury road. There was Manston, a tiny patch of light green.

Altitude eight thousand feet. To hell with it, this would have to do. The noses of the Messerschmitts went down and the fighters howled earthwards. Some flak started to come up, but it was a long way off to the right.

There was no point in keeping radio silence now. Richter ordered his flight to spread out and adopt a line-abreast attack formation, following the example of Number One Flight, a few hundred yards ahead.

On Manston airfield, a flight of Spitfires was taxiing out for take off, swerving round the bomb craters left by an air attack earlier in the day. A second flight had just begun to move when the leading Messerschmitts screamed over the airfield, firing with everything they had.

Richter saw Major Hartwig's aircraft overhauling a Spitfire that was making a desperate attempt to get airborne, bumping across the grass. Hartwig fired, and the British fighter disintegrated in a cloud of burning fuel and debris. The Messerschmitt raced through the spreading cloud of smoke, putting a burst of fire through the open door of a hangar before climbing away steeply, followed by the other four aircraft of the leading flight.

Richter sighted on another Spitfire as he levelled out and streaked across the pitted surface of the airfield at twenty feet. The Messerschmitt shuddered with the recoil of its cannon and machine-guns. One of the Spitfire's undercarriage legs folded up suddenly and the fighter's wingtip ploughed into the ground. The Spitfire slewed round in a half-circle and came to a stop. Richter saw the pilot jump clear as he raced past. He squirted a fuel bowser, which exploded in a balloon of fire, then pulled back the stick and sent his Messerschmitt leaping into the sky.

He went up to five thousand feet and turned, glancing to left and right. The other aircraft of his flight were still with him, like faithful hounds.

'All right, one more run and we'll get the hell out of it.'

They pushed their noses down. Ahead of them, Hartwig's aircraft were already making their second pass, cleaving through the spreading pall of smoke that shrouded half the airfield. The Tommies had woken up at last and flak was coming up thick and fast now, Bofors guns around the perimeter hurling glowing strings of shells at the speeding German fighters. Richter saw a Messerschmitt, the number four aircraft in the leading flight, suddenly stream flames from its port wing and hit the ground. It bounced high in the air and then cartwheeled across the field, shedding fragments as it went.

With all the smoke, it was difficult to pick out a worthwhile target. A truck crossed Richter's nose and he fired a short burst at it. His shells churned up puffs of dust as they converged on the vehicle. Flashes twinkled over it and it veered away sharply, still moving at speed. An aircraft appeared out of the smoke, coming at him head-on. He fired and missed. Just as well; the aircraft was a Messerschmitt. It missed him by a hair's breadth and vanished.

The Messerschmitts raced for the coast, the checkerboard fields of Kent flashing beneath them. Suddenly, three miles north of Dover, a warning shout crackled over the radio from an aircraft in Number Three Flight: 'Spitfires coming in astern!'

Richter craned his neck, searching the sky above and behind. There they were, a whole avalanche of them, coming out of the sun. Not Spitfires but Hurricanes – however, it made little difference. They were already tearing into Number Three Flight.

He glanced at his fuel gauge, assessing the situation rapidly. Number One Flight was already out to sea and clear of the danger, but if he chose to run for it the Hurricanes, with their height and speed advantage, would shoot the Messerschmitts to pieces before they had a chance to escape. There was only one alternative. Richter pressed the R/T button.

'Form a defensive circle.'

It was the standard tactic used by twin-engined Messerschmitt 110s when they were hard-pressed, but Richter saw no reason why it should not work for his single-engined fighters too. In the defensive circle, each aircraft would be able to cover the one in front. In this way, they could keep the Tommies at bay until they were in a position to run for it.

Richter crammed on more power and started to turn, the other 109s jockeying into position behind him with a hundred yards between each aircraft. He was still turning hard when a stream of tracer knifed past his wingtip, followed closely by a Hurricane. Two more Hurricanes converged on the rearmost aircraft of Richter's flight, which was lagging some distance behind the rest; a moment later the Messerschmitt was fluttering down, torn in half. There was no sign of a parachute.

The four remaining 109s completed their circle. It was all they could do to hold their own. The Hurricanes ripped through them time and again, and it was as much as the Germans could do to get in an occasional burst as the British fighters zoomed past. Richter got off one lucky shot; a Hurricane faltered and broke off the attack, diving away and trailing a thin streamer of smoke.

A second Messerschmitt went down, breaking up as it fell. Richter knew that he and the two surviving machines had to make a break for it soon, or they would be overwhelmed by sheer weight of numbers. Either that, or their fuel would run out halfway across the Channel.

The Hurricanes drew away in readiness for another assault, and he saw his chance. He yelled: 'Run like hell!' over the radio and pushed down his fighter's nose, levelling out a few feet over the Channel, closely followed by the other 109s. The Hurricanes pursued them for some distance, firing at extreme range, then broke off the attack and turned inland once more.

In a field near the southern outskirts of Dover, soldiers and civilians clustered round a smoking crater. An eyewitness was explaining excitedly how a Messerschmitt had dived into the ground vertically, shot down by two Hurricanes after a tremendous dogfight.

There was nothing left of the pilot but a fragment of shinbone. A soldier, combing through the scattered wreckage around the crater, picked up something from the grass; it was a silver hip-flask, blackened by flames. He wiped it on his sleeve and a name showed up faintly, engraved in the metal. He could make out only the initial letters, F. P.

He glanced round covertly to see if anyone was looking, then slipped the flask into his pocket. It would make a fine souvenir.

Chapter Three

THE PILOTS OF 505 SQUADRON HAD BEEN AT READI-
ness since eight o'clock. Now, five hours later, they were
getting bored. It was two days since the start of the
German air offensive, but so far all the action had been
confined to the south, in the domain of Fighter Command's Eleven and Twelve Groups, leaving the reserve
squadrons of Thirteen Group to play a waiting game.

The waiting could not go on much longer; everyone
knew that. The southern squadrons had already taken a
mauling. On paper, Fighter Command had come out on
top in the battles of Eagle Day, destroying forty-five
enemy aircraft for the loss of thirteen Spitfires and Hurricanes; but many more British fighters had been damaged,
putting them out of action for some time. Together with
the twenty-two fighters which had been lost the day
before, it all added up to a rate of attrition which could
not be sustained for long.

Bad weather had frustrated the Luftwaffe's plans on
the fourteenth, and the weather reports had indicated
that the following day would be equally unpromising.
Daybreak on the fifteenth had revealed a grey overcast,
stretching without a break over most of the British Isles.

Then, quite unexpectedly, the clouds had begun to
disperse shortly after ten o'clock, and the Luftwaffe had
seized its opportunity. Forty Stukas, strongly escorted by
Messerschmitts, had swept across the Channel and hit
Eleven Group's airfields of Lympne and Hawkinge, putting the former completely out of action.

Yeoman lounged in a deckchair outside the dispersal hut, reading a book. From time to time, he chuckled out loud. The sound disturbed Jim Callender, who was playing pontoon with three more pilots.

'What are you reading that's so funny?' he asked, looking up. '*The Manual of Air Force Law*?'

Yeoman laid his book aside and stretched. 'No, as a matter of fact it's *The Wind in the Willows*. One of my all-time favourites. Every time I read it, I find something new in it.' He grinned. 'Actually, I was laughing because I was identifying Ratty and Mole and Toad with some of you types. I'm not saying who was who.'

One of the pontoon players, a dark-haired flight sergeant pilot named Simon Wynne-Williams – a veteran of the French Campaign, like Yeoman and Callender – looked in mock bewilderment from one to the other.

'What's he talking about?' he asked. Wynne-Williams had not read *The Wind in the Willows*. Neither, apparently, had Callender.

'Search me,' he said. 'I think he's entering his second childhood.'

'He never emerged from his first, if you ask me,' said the other.

'Ah, me,' said Yeoman, assuming a long-suffering expression, 'what a burden it is to have to share my existence with peasants and philistines.'

'I think,' said Callender, getting up slowly, 'that a remark like that is going to cost you your pants.' He moved menacingly towards his laughing colleague, followed by Wynne-Williams.

The ops telephone shrilled and they all froze, looking expectantly at the open door of the hut. A moment later Hillier burst out, struggling into his Mae West lifejacket, yelling at the top of his voice.

'Scramble! Angels Twelve, over the Tyne. There's a big gaggle coming in!'

Cards, books, magazines and chairs went flying as they

ran for their Spitfires, whooping and yelling like school-boys. Yeoman's parachute lay on the wing of his aircraft and he buckled it on while a mechanic started the engine. The Merlin coughed into life in a cloud of blue smoke and the mechanic scrambled out of the bucket seat, making way for its rightful occupant.

Yeoman swung his leg over the cockpit side-flap and lowered himself into the seat, his parachute forming a cushion under him. He fastened the Sutton harness, closed the flap and plugged in his R/T lead. A mechanic unplugged the starter battery, closed the flap on the side of the engine cowling and gave Yeoman a thumbs-up.

On paper, 505 Squadron was up to its full complement of twenty fighters; some, however, were unserviceable and others were undergoing routine servicing, so that the unit's full flying strength was twelve Spitfires. These were split into two flights, 'A' and 'B', and each flight in turn was sub-divided into two sections. 'A' Flight provided Red and Yellow Sections, 'B' Flight Blue and Green. Yeoman, leading Blue Section, was Blue One. His wing-men, a sergeant pilot named Keenan and a very young and inexperienced pilot officer, Hamilton, were Blue Two and Blue Three respectively.

Yeoman mentally went through his cockpit checks. BTFCPPUR – Brakes, Trim, Flaps, Contacts, Pressure, Petrol, Undercarriage, Radiator. All okay. The six Spits of 'A' Flight were already taxiing out. Time to go. A quick look round, and a thumbs-up from Hamilton and Keenan. Handbrake off, a touch of throttle and the Spit-fire began to roll forward, bumping slowly across the grass, rolling on its narrow-track undercarriage as Yeo-man applied coarse left and right rudder alternately, yawing the long nose from side to side to clear the blind spot directly in front of it. He wrinkled his nose; the cockpit reeked of glycol as usual.

He made a final cockpit check, as he taxied out and turned into wind. Some pilots skipped them, and some pilots ended up dead. It was little use getting off the ground in a hurry only to have your engine pack up in a dogfight because you hadn't bothered to check the oil temperature.

RAFTS. R for retractable undercart, green light on. A for airscrew in fine pitch. F for flaps up. T for trim, just a little aft of centre on the wheel in the cockpit. S for Sperry gyro, caged. Another quick look round; nothing above and behind. A hand signal to his two wingmen and he pushed the throttle wide open as he turned into wind, sending the Spitfire lurching forward across the field. Stick forward a little to lift the tail, but not too far or the long propeller blades would dig into the ground.

The Spitfire bounced two or three times and then became airborne. Yeoman selected 'undercarriage up', briefly thanking God and Supermarine for the automatic retraction system that had replaced the laborious pump-handle method of earlier marks. He settled down into a steady climb, reaching up and closing the cockpit hood.

'Hello, Blackbird, Stingray airborne.' That was Hillier, making contact with control.

'Roger, Stingray, vector 010, Angels one five now. Patrol Tynemouth and await instructions. Estimate sixty plus bandits twenty miles out, Angels twelve, course 190.'

Sixty plus. If radar was correct, this was a really big one – the biggest raid to hit the north of England so far. Yeoman wondered what they were after. It must be the Tyne shipyards, and probably the airfields in Northumberland and Durham.

The twelve Spitfires went up quickly to fifteen thousand feet, slicing through the broken cloud that hung over the coast. The broad estuary of the Tyne and the sprawling complex of Newcastle, seen dimly through a veil of industrial haze, was below and to the left. Yeoman picked out the wake of a large ship, something at least the size of a cruiser, forging out to sea between the north and south piers.

He made another check around the cockpit and, satisfied that everything was as it should be, switched on his reflector sight. The red circle and dot appeared as if by magic on the bullet-proof glass in the centre of his windshield. His finger stroked the milled wheel of the safety catch; all he had to do was turn it to 'fire', press the button and his eight ·303 Brownings would roar out, hammering eight thousand rounds per minute – or 266 rounds in an average two-second burst – into an area two feet in diameter 250 yards in front of the nose. It was enough to punch a sizeable and, hopefully, fatal hole in the wings or fuselage of an enemy aircraft, even if the burst missed a more vital spot such as the engine. Two of the eight guns were loaded with armour-piercing ammunition, two with incendiary and four with ball. Four out of the last twenty-five rounds in each box of ball ammunition were tracer, to warn the pilot that his firepower was running out. In the port wing root, a synchronized G42 film camera waited to record the results of the pilot's shooting.

'Hello, Blackbird, Stingray calling. Orbiting Tynemouth, Angels fifteen. Any gen?'

'Roger, Stingray, bandits over Blyth, now heading 180, Angels twelve, confirmed sixty plus. Vector 350 to intercept.'

The Spitfires swept round in a wide arc, re-crossing the coast and heading north. So much for the 'twenty miles out' bit, thought Yeoman. The radar, sometimes notoriously inaccurate, must have been playing tricks again.

'There the bastards are, eleven o'clock!'

Yeoman scanned the horizon, and saw the enemy almost at once: a great cloud of dots spread out across the sky, scudding along over the mass of broken cloud. 'Sixty plus' had been a very conservative estimate. There must be at least a hundred of them.

'Ker-rist!' Yeoman recognized Jim Callender's drawl.

'All right,' Hillier snapped, 'cut the cackle. Blue and Green Sections, upstairs. Red and Yellow, with me. Head-on attack.'

The six Spitfires of Blue and Green Sections went up to eighteen thousand feet, searching the sky above the enemy bombers. The latter were identifiable as Heinkel 111s, and speckled across the sky above and to either side of them were groups of smaller dots which must be their fighter escort. For a minute Yeoman was puzzled. The bombers were coming from the north-east, presumably from Norway, and the Messerschmitt 109 did not have sufficient range to undertake the long haul over the North Sea. Then he realized that the fighters were not 109s at all; they were twin-engined 110s.

The enemy formation seemed dislocated. In fact they had already been in action, intercepted over the Farne Islands by a squadron of Hurricanes from Acklington. The Hurricanes had tangled with the Messerschmitt 110 escort and had come out decidedly on top. Several 110s had been either shot down or damaged, and others had fled for home.

The bombers, however, had continued steadily on their course, escorted by the surviving 110s, and now Hillier's small force of Spitfires was all that stood between them and the vital Tyne shipyards. At least the British fighters, coming out of the south-east, had the sun in their favour.

While 'A' Flight went for the bombers, Blue and Green Sections of 'B' Flight split up, manœuvring to attack the Messerschmitt escort from different angles. Yeoman led his Blue Section towards four 110s on the left flank of the bomber formation, the Spitfires diving hard from the beam.

The Huns showed every inclination to fight, turning to meet the Spitfires head-on. As they did so, Yeoman saw four black objects, like teardrops, fall away from under the Messerschmitts' bellies and go fluttering down. So that's how they step up the range, he thought; auxiliary fuel tanks.

The 110s split up into two pairs, one of them suddenly climbing to the left to take the Spits in the flank. They ran full tilt into the aircraft of Green Section, sweeping down unobserved out of the glare, and suddenly found themselves fighting desperately for their lives. Yeoman lost sight of them as the other two 110s came hard at his section, their noses twinkling with the flash of their cannon. He fired back, cringing as the smoke trails from the enemy fighter's guns seemed to converge on a spot between his eyes, but the 110's shells streaked over the top of Yeoman's cockpit and the next instant the fighter was gone, buffeting the Spitfire with its slipstream as it flashed underneath.

'I'm hit! Christ, I'm hit!' Hamilton's shrill, panic-stricken voice burst over the radio. Yeoman turned hard, looking back. Blue Two, Sergeant Keenan, was still with him. A mile away, a parabola of black smoke curved down into the clouds. Yeoman pressed the R/T button.

'Blue Three from Blue One, are you okay? Blue Three, come in. Are you okay?'

There was no answer. Slowly, the streamer of smoke began to disperse on the wind. Beyond it, two black dots that were the 110s were high-tailing it out to sea. There was no sign of the other two.

'All right, Blue Two, leave 'em. Let's get after the bombers.'

Keenan acknowledged briefly and the two Spitfires turned southwards, scudding along over the clouds. Yeoman searched the horizon. Not for the first time, he marvelled at the sheer speed of air combat, and at the vast scope of the sky. One moment the sky would be full of whirling aircraft; the next it would be empty. This, he knew, was the dangerous time, the moment when a pilot, fresh from the exertions of combat, was tempted to relax for a moment – and leave himself wide open to an enemy fighter, arrowing unseen out of the sun.

Apart from himself and his wingman the sky seemed quite deserted, but a lot of shouting was going on over the radio and the air battle must still be raging further south. He told Keenan to keep his eyes peeled, then switched to another channel and called up control.

'Hello, Blackbird, Stingray Blue One calling. Requesting vector.'

'Roger, Stingray Blue One, transmit.'

'Stingray Blue One transmitting, one . . . two . . . three . . . four . . . five.'

There was a momentary silence. Then: 'Stingray Blue One from Blackbird, vector 160. Bogeys over Tynemouth heading 190. Switch to Channel "A". Buster.'

'Buster' meant get a move on. Yeoman and Keenan opened their throttles and turned on to the heading that had been given to them. It was Keenan who spotted the enemy first, a widely spaced trio of twin-engined machines popping up out of the clouds a couple of miles ahead. His yell almost shattered Yeoman's eardrums.

The aircraft were Junkers 88s, and they were fast. Even at full throttle, the Spitfires had their work cut out to overhaul them. Black smoke trails streamed from the 88s' engines as the enemy pilots crammed on power.

Yeoman selected the left-hand bomber and went into a shallow dive, gaining speed and coming up from astern and slightly underneath. The 88's ventral gunner opened up, but his shots were wild. Yeoman opened fire too, but the range was too great. He cursed himself for acting like a bloody beginner and crept in closer, his thumb resting lightly on the button. Tracer floated from the Junkers in orange clusters, moving apparently slowly and then separating and flashing around the Spitfire like deadly wasps.

Yeoman's thumb jabbed down and a two-second burst pumped into the 88's fuselage. There was no apparent effect; the enemy bomber flew on steadily. There was a sudden loud banging noise, like a hammer beating on a drum, and holes appeared in the Spit's starboard wing. He kicked the rudder and the fighter skidded out of the line of fire. Sweat trickled in rivulets down the sides of his nose and he wiped it away with his sleeve. That had been too close for comfort.

Keenan called up, his voice filled with disgust and frustration. 'Blue Two to Blue One – my bloody engine's boiling. Breaking off. My 88's pissed off into the clouds.'

Yeoman acknowledged and glanced back. The bomber in front of him was the only aircraft still in sight. A rift in the clouds revealed a city over on the right, with a river looping tightly through its heart. From the peninsula girded by the river, a solid, angular tower jutted up. He had no trouble in identifying Durham.

The 88 was still heading south at full throttle. He closed in again, this time from above and behind, and put another burst into the fuselage just behind the cockpit. A slight touch of rudder and bullets ploughed into the bomber's left wing, between engine and fuselage. Yeoman swore fluently; the bastard refused to burn. More tracer converged on his fighter, causing him to swerve violently aside once more.

Suddenly, the Junkers dropped like a stone, plunging into the cloud layer fifteen hundred feet lower down. Yeoman throttled back rapidly and followed suit. He glanced at his altimeter; nine thousand feet. He had no idea what the Junkers might be up to; all he could do was hold a straight course and hope for the best.

He broke through the cloud base at four thousand feet, over the outskirts of a town. Three tall chimneys and the squatter shapes of cooling towers close by them dominated the familiar skyline of Darlington. On a sudden impulse he looked up at the grey cloud layer, streaming just a few feet above his cockpit canopy. Hanging there, surrounded by a rainbow-like halo, was the ghostly shadow of the Junkers, almost directly overhead.

35

Hardly daring to believe his good fortune, Yeoman reduced speed. The shadow crept ahead, and then abruptly the Junkers popped out of the cloud and hung there, a sitting target squarely in his sights. He saw every detail in a single, vivid flash; the bottle-green camouflage of the upper surfaces, the pale grey belly, the stark black crosses.

He fired, sighting carefully on the bomber's port engine. A large piece of metal broke off and whirled past him. A thin trail of white smoke streamed back, but there were no flames.

The Junker's bomb-doors swung open and a stick of bombs tumbled out. Yeoman, close enough almost to touch the 88, pulled aside violently, cold with fear as the falling missiles arc'd past his wingtip. The bomber, lightened of its load, shot up into the sheltering clouds once more.

Yeoman saw the bombs curve down and explode in a field just outside the town, a hundred yards away from some farm buildings. A few seconds earlier, and they would have erupted right in the town centre.

He looked at his fuel gauge. He had very little left – certainly not enough to search for the Junkers any more. His radio had gone suddenly dead, into the bargain. He turned south-west, following the line of the Great North Road. With Scotch Corner over on his right wingtip he looked ahead, seeking out the grass expanse and camou-flaged hangars of Catterick airfield. He located it without difficulty and flew overhead at two thousand feet, drop-ping neatly into the circuit. A pair of Spitfires were ahead of him and more behind; Catterick's fighter squadrons had been in action and were returning to base. No one seemed to be taking the blindest bit of notice of the light signals that were being flashed from the runway con-troller's caravan; Spitfires and Hurricanes were landing all over the place.

All right. Speed downwind 180 miles per hour, just

right. Propeller to fine pitch; undercart down. A reassuring thump. Turn across wind, curving continuously to keep the touchdown point in sight. Flaps down. A hiss of compressed air, a drop of the nose. Trim back for a power-on approach, not too much. Hood open, bringing a welcome rush of air against sweaty cheeks and forehead. Keep the turn going into wind. Ninety miles per hour over the fence; a slight drop as the Spitfire crossed the river and a touch of power to correct the sink. Level out, throttle back and hold off. A bump as the wheels touched, a slight bounce and then the Spit was down for good, out of her element once more. Not a three-pointer, but good enough.

Yeoman raised his flaps and taxied towards the flight huts, following other Spitfires. An airman appeared in front of him, arms upraised, marshalling him in. He joined the line of Spitfires, some of them with their propellers still turning, and braked gently to a stop. He applied the handbrake and pulled the slow-running cut-out ring. The engine, starved of fuel, coughed a few times and then was silent.

He levered himself stiffly out of the cockpit, leaving his parachute where it was, and jumped down off the wing. He suddenly realized that he was soaked in sweat from head to foot.

He went into operations, made his report to the duty officer, and telephoned Usworth with news of his whereabouts. He asked about Hamilton, but no one knew what had become of him. He wandered outside again and sat on the grass, watching ground crews swarming over the fighters. After a while, some of the pilots who had just returned came and flopped down on the grass nearby to await the arrival of the van bearing their tea and sandwiches. Yeoman fell into conversation with them, and gradually built up a picture of the raid he had helped to break up just a short while ago.

The German bombers, clearly hoping that most of

Fighter Command would be tied up over southern England, had hit the north in two waves. The first, composed of the Heinkels of Bomber Wing 26 with their Messerschmitt escort, had made landfall about seventy miles too far north, and had been harried in turn by squadrons of Spitfires and Hurricanes, as well as anti-aircraft defences all along the coast. They had dropped their bombs more or less at random over the eastern part of Durham County. Eight Heinkels and six 110s had been shot down.

The second wave, three squadrons of fast Junkers 88s with no fighter escort, had come in over the Yorkshire coast. It was three stragglers from this raid, apparently, which Yeoman had encountered. They had been slightly more fortunate in that they had reached their objectives and had caused severe damage at Driffield, a bomber airfield north of the Humber. Nevertheless, they had been engaged by Spitfires and Hurricanes from Church Fenton, and six of them had been destroyed.

Yeoman wandered over to check the state of his Spitfire. Riggers were patching up the bullet holes in the wing, which fortunately had not caused serious damage. The aircraft would be ready to fly away in about an hour. Reassured, he wandered back to the flight huts in time to catch the NAAFI van and a welcome mug of tea. He toyed with the idea of going off to the sergeants' mess for lunch, then decided against it. A sandwich would do for now.

He heard someone call his name and looked round, startled. A young pilot officer was striding towards him across the grass. Yeoman recognized him at once; his name was Fred Kirby. They had gone through the fighter conversion course together several months earlier. Six months to be exact, thought Yeoman with a shock; it seemed almost like a lifetime.

The two men shook hands warmly. 'Well, Fred,' Yeoman grinned, 'I see you've acquired a cat's whisker.' He was referring to Kirby's solitary thin blue stripe. 'I suppose that means I've got to call you sir, or something.'

'Something'll do,' Kirby replied. 'I always thought you'd have been commissioned before me. What happened?'

Yeoman shrugged. 'I reckon I've been a bit too busy to think about it. It looks as though the Powers are going to catch up with me though, because I'm in for one. I was boarded a couple of weeks ago. I'm not sure whether it's the right thing to do. Officers don't eat peas off their knives for a start.'

'You ought to see some of our bunch,' Kirby laughed. 'Hey, it really is good to see you. I thought you'd bought it over Dunkirk. I made a few enquiries about you among your lot at Manston at the end of May, but they said you were missing. I must have just missed you. Was it rough?'

Yeoman nodded. 'Rough enough. Let's just say I was very glad to get out of it, and that a million quid wouldn't entice me to join the poor bloody infantry. What they went through over there was nobody's business.' He recalled the incident in the pub, a couple of days earlier, and shuddered inwardly.

He pulled a pipe and tobacco pouch from his pocket, and packed the bowl carefully. About a month earlier he had suddenly felt the urge to smoke; he had tried a cigarette and thrown it away in disgust, but he had taken to a pipe almost straight away. He didn't smoke excessively; a couple of fills a day were enough. He found it an excellent aid to relaxation.

He paused and looked at Kirby. 'What about you? You went off to 32 Squadron, didn't you? That was the last I heard of you.'

'That's right. We got knocked about a bit during the Dunkirk show, and just got up to strength again in time for Jerry's attacks on the Channel convoys. That was quite a merry-go-round, but I think we came out on top. We really hammered the Stukas. The trouble was that we never operated in sufficient strength to tackle both the Hun bombers and their fighter escort successfully.'

39

Yeoman nodded, lighting his pipe. 'So I heard. By the way, do you remember Alan Porter? He went on to Defiants, poor bastard – 141 Squadron, I think, I bumped into him at Church Fenton a few weeks ago. He was a nervous wreck. Lost most of the squadron when the Huns bounced them over Dover. Just imagine – sitting in front of a bloody silly gun turret, with somebody else doing all the shooting, and no front guns at all!'

'God, yes! Anyway, I hear they've pulled the Defiants off daylight ops altogether. Somebody said they're turning them into night-fighters. We're going to need a few of those, too; if we maul Jerry enough during the day he'll start coming over in strength after dark, and as it is we've got nothing to stop him.'

Yeoman grunted. 'Same old story. I don't suppose it would be much of a picnic, stooging around at night over London or somewhere with all that ack-ack belting away. They can't tell the difference between us and the Huns in broad daylight, as it is.' He looked thoughtful, drawing on his pipe. 'Still,' he continued, 'it would be a bit of a challenge. I wouldn't mind having a go at night-fighters, if it meant more chances to have a bash at the bombers. So long as the night-fighters weren't bloody Defiants, that is.'

An NCO stuck his head out of one of the hut windows and shouted for Pilot Officer Kirby. The latter slapped Yeoman on the shoulder.

'Well, George, I'm on my way. I came up here in a Magister to collect a replacement flight commander. It looks as though he's ready for off.'

'All right, Fred. See you around. We'll have a beer down in the fleshpots sometime.'

They never did. Four days later, Kirby was shot down in flames over Beachy Head. His hood was jammed and he was unable to bale out. His radio was switched to transmit and his screams jammed the frequency for the endless terrible forty-five seconds it took him to fall from seventeen thousand feet.

Chapter Four

RICHTER HAD NEVER SEEN SO MANY BOMBERS IN THE same bit of sky. There were at least two hundred of them, flying in two waves. The first wave, strung out like a swarm of locusts across the horizon, was composed of Junkers 87 Stukas; the second, bringing up the rear, of Junkers 88s. The fighters were up in strength, too; elements of four fighter wings, dancing like silvery midges over the armada as it headed towards the English coast.

It was five o'clock in the afternoon of 15 August. Once again, the RAF airfields in southern England – already badly hit by a series of Luftwaffe raids earlier in the day – were the target. According to Intelligence, much of Fighter Command's resources had already been destroyed on the ground. The Luftwaffe crews had been told that they could expect little opposition to this, the final major raid of the day.

Richter wasn't so sure. Earlier in the day, Fighter Wing 66 had escorted a squadron of Dorniers in an attack on the RAF airfield at Eastchurch and an aircraft factory near Rochester, and the pilots had not sighted a single British fighter – but that, thought Richter, didn't mean they no longer existed. He knew that other raids had been in progress all over southern England, and was inclined to believe that the RAF had been busy dealing with these. With all the bombers and their fighter escort concentrated in one patch of sky, as they were now, it might well be a different story. None of the German pilots, moreover, could understand why almost the whole afternoon had been allowed to go by with no follow-up attacks.

'General Kesselring and General Sperrle again,' Major Hartwig had observed cynically, 'tearing each other's eyes out and fighting over whose air fleet is going to bomb what, no doubt. And by the time they sort themselves out, the Tommies are waiting for us again with their claws sharpened. I'd like to get the whole Luftwaffe High Command together and boot them out over England – without parachutes. They're far more dangerous to us than they are to the Tommies.'

Hartwig was right; but, as his colleague Major Meurer told him quietly, it wasn't the kind of opinion one voiced too loudly. Walls not only had ears in the Third Reich; they also had a nasty habit of swallowing people up.

One thing was certain; the afternoon's delay had cost the Luftwaffe its tactical advantage. Already, as the bombers and their fighter escort approached the English coast, fourteen squadrons of Spitfires and Hurricanes – 170 fighters in all – were climbing hard to meet them. The fighter controllers, recalling their earlier experience when the fighter squadrons had been scattered piecemeal to counter a dozen smaller attacks, had at first been wary of committing most of their available strength to one sector – but now it seemed certain that the enemy bombers were not going to break formation and head for a series of separate targets. It was the opportunity for which Fighter Command had been waiting.

Richter, whose fighter wing was escorting the Junkers 88 formation, heard the radio suddenly come alive with shouts and curses as the first Spitfires and Hurricanes clashed with the Stukas high over the coast. Before long, it was clear that the bombers were having a hard time of it.

Still, that was someone else's problem. The Junkers 88 formation was over the Isle of Wight when it encountered problems of its own.

'Fighters attacking from astern. Coming in from above!'

Richter and the other fighter pilots, weaving several thousand feet higher up, looked down as they heard the warning call from one of the bombers. Apart from the Junkers formation, the sky over the coast seemed empty. Where the hell were the Tommies?

He saw them quite suddenly, a string of glittering pearls hurtling through the bomber formation from the seaward side. They must have manœuvred out over the Channel to get the sun behind them.

Colonel Becker's clipped voice came over the R/T. 'Attention! Two and Three Squadrons, close escort. One Squadron, top cover. Attack! Attack!'

Like a shoal of fish, the thirty Messerschmitts of Fighter Wing 66's Numbers Two and Three Squadrons plummeted to the rescue of the bombers. Above them, the remaining squadron turned to face a dozen Spitfires, sweeping down from the north.

The hard-pressed bombers had closed up their formation in an attempt to improve their collective fire-cover. A pack of Spitfires worried at their heels, harrying the rearmost flight of Junkers. Richter saw one of them, its port engine in flames, suddenly break up in mid-air. Its wing folded back in a cascade of sparks and the bomber fell out of the sky, trailing streamers of burning fuel.

The Messerschmitts, diving at full throttle though they were, arrived too late to save four Junkers 88s. Two and a half miles below, their wreckage burned in the Hampshire countryside.

Richter levelled out, glancing back as he did so. His wingman, Sergeant Brandtner, was in position a couple of hundred yards astern, high to the right. Reassured, Richter looked ahead in search of a target. The sky was full of fighters, whirling in a gigantic free-for-all around the Junkers formation. A Hurricane flashed across his nose; he fired and missed.

With all the shouting going on over the radio, it was difficult to concentrate. 'Hawks in the sun . . . Hawks in the sun, high to port . . . Victor, victor, I have contact . . . Elbe Leader from Elbe Three, two Spitfires behind you . . . Help! The swine are shooting me down . . . I got that one. Did you see? I got him! Three Squadron, Three Squadron, come on down, damn you! Where are you? . . . Siegfried Two to Siegfried Leader, more Hawks on your starboard quarter, high. . . .'

Suddenly, Richter heard Brandtner's excited voice cut through the babble. 'Gustav One from Gustav Two. Spitfire astern and to starboard, closing in! Range one thousand metres.'

'Victor, Gustav Two. Watch him.' Richter knew that the British fighter pilots liked to get in as close as possible before opening fire, to make more certain of a 'kill'. This Tommy was obviously so intent on shooting down Richter that he had failed to see Brandtner, lurking in the sky to starboard.

He could see the shark-like front view of the Spitfire in his rear-view mirror, closing rapidly in a shallow dive. Mentally, he ticked off the range. Seven hundred metres . . . five hundred. Wait for it – now! He heard Brandtner yell 'Break!' and at that same instant he kicked the rudder bar and pulled the stick hard into his right thigh. Short contrails streamed from the Messerschmitt's wing-tips as it flipped into a steep turn. The Spitfire, its pilot taken completely by surprise by the sudden manœuvre, shot past, its speed too high to follow suit.

Richter pulled the stick back into the pit of his stomach, opening the throttle and turning hard through 360 degrees. The 109 juddered slightly; sustained steep turns at high speed were hard work because of the little brute's high wing loading, and it was likely to flick into a spin at the drop of a hat.

He rolled out of the turn. Brandtner had passed him and was chasing the Spitfire, which was about a mile ahead. The British pilot maintained his shallow dive, which was a mistake on his part, because in a dive the

Messerschmitt was faster. Richter, closing the distance rapidly, saw dark grey smoke trails stream back in the wake of Brandtner's Messerschmitt as his wingman opened fire. The Spitfire curved away in a turn to the left, and Richter altered his heading to cut it off. He fired as the distinctive, elliptical-winged silhouette came into his sights, and the Spitfire abruptly turned the other way – into Brandtner's line of fire.

There was a flash, and a tiny pinpoint of flame appeared at the Spitfire's wing root. It grew into a long streamer, flowing along the side of the fuselage. Richter lined up and fired in turn, and the British fighter went into a steep climb, belching smoke. It lost speed, stalled and went into a spin, a black corkscrew of smoke marking its fall. Richter, looking down, saw a vivid splash of fire, instantly extinguished, where it hit the ground far below.

Colonel Becker's voice came over the R/T, calling on the wing to re-form. The Junkers 88s were already over their targets, the airfields of Worthy Down and Middle Wallop. The two RAF fighter squadrons on the latter, a vital sector station, escaped destruction by seconds. The last Spitfires were just taking off when the first German bombs exploded among the hangars behind them.

Section by section, the 109s of Fighter Wing 66 converged on the rendezvous, just to the east of Southampton. The wing was only partly re-formed when more warning shouts burst over the radio. Richter scanned the northern sky, and his heart missed a beat. A swarm of British fighters, at least three squadrons, was heading flat out for the circling Messerschmitts. They were Hurricanes, and they had height in their favour. The 109s scattered in all directions, like bees in a disturbed hive, as the Hurricanes sailed in among them. The British pilots were making the most of their initial height and speed advantage; once that was lost, the Hurricane was inferior to the 109 on most counts.

The events of the next few minutes were to remain

totally confused in Richter's mind. Tactics were thrown to the winds; it was every man for himself. A 109 exploded and went down vertically, a ball of fire that broke apart as it fell. A Hurricane flicked past, minus a wing and rolling over and over. A parachute blossomed out, then collapsed again at once. Richter got a shot at a Hurricane and saw his bullets stitch a pattern across the fighter's roundel, just behind the cockpit. It was gone before he had a chance to fire again.

Several of the German pilots, including Richter and Brandtner, desperately tried to form a defensive circle. It was their only chance of survival; they did not have enough fuel left for prolonged combat. Their only chance was to keep on corkscrewing across the sky in this hellish merry-go-round, then make a break for it when they spotted an opening.

The whole Royal Air Force seemed to be in action today! A shoal of fighters, Spitfires this time, dived slap through the middle of the defensive circle, disrupting it momentarily as the startled German pilots turned to meet what they thought was a new threat. But the Spitfires continued their dive, streaking over the coast in pursuit of their real target: the retreating Junkers 88s.

There was nothing the fighter pilots could do to help the bombers. Two more Messerschmitts were already going down in flames. Others, their fuel dangerously low and their ammunition exhausted, took a chance and ran for it, diving away into the thin heat haze that hung over the Channel.

The fight was not all one-sided. A Hurricane, its pilot somewhat over-confident, suddenly dropped into the defensive circle and opened fire on the 109 in front of Richter. The latter could hardly believe his eyes. He took a deep breath and lined up his sights carefully on the spot where the Hurricane's wing joined the fuselage, just below the cockpit. His guns hammered briefly, then stopped abruptly as his ammunition ran out.

46

The single burst was enough. A great sheet of metal ripped away from the Hurricane's wing root and Richter's bullets tore off a large section of the fuselage's fabric covering, punching the wooden spars to splinters. The wing folded up and broke free, whirling past Richter's cockpit. The rest of the Hurricane went over on its back and dropped like a stone.

Richter looked around quickly. There seemed to be a momentary lull in the battle. It was now or never. He called up Brandtner and they pushed down the noses of their fighters, heading out over the sea at full throttle.

'Gustav Two to Gustav One. I think I've been hit.'

Richter turned his head, searching for Brandtner's aircraft. He located it a thousand feet below him, astern and to the right. It was pouring smoke.

'Gustav Two, you're on fire. Bale out. I repeat, bale out.'

'No, I'm staying with it. Too close to Tommyland . . . I don't want to be taken prisoner.' Brandtner's voice was high-pitched and strained.

Richter spoke to him urgently. 'Brandtner, don't be a bloody fool. She'll go up at any moment. Get out while you can. I order you to get out!'

'Sir, with respect, you can stuff your orders. I can hold her for a little while longer . . . long enough to get a bit further out over the Ditch.'

Brandtner's Messerschmitt flew on, shrouded in smoke, losing height all the time. Richter throttled back, keeping pace with it. He kept glancing anxiously at his fuel gauge; he hoped it was inaccurate and that he had more petrol left than it showed, otherwise he wouldn't make it.

The French coast was visible now, a thin line in the haze. The two 109s were heading for the Cherbourg Peninsula; there was no hope whatsoever of regaining Abbeville.

Richter looked down. His wingman's Messerschmitt

was almost brushing the waves. The red glow of flames showed through the smoke.

Brandtner's voice came again, weak and broken by racking coughs.

'Hello, Gustav One, can't see a thing . . . cockpit full of smoke. Can't see to ditch . . . am baling out.'

'Brandtner,' Richter yelled, 'don't be a bloody fool! You're too low! I repeat, do *not* try to bale out!'

There was no answer. Instead, the square-cut cockpit hood of Brandtner's Messerschmitt fell away and Richter saw the pilot's head and shoulders emerge, blurred among all the smoke. The next instant, the dark shape of Brandtner's body was plucked clear, sprawling along the side of the fuselage and missing the tailplane by inches.

Richter found himself shouting incoherently over the radio, praying at the top of his voice for Brandtner's parachute to open. With a gasp of relief, he saw a yellow streamer of silk flow out in the wake of the tumbling black speck that was his wingman's body.

A split second later, with the parachute only half deployed, Brandtner hit the sea.

Richter circled the spot once. There was no sign of the pilot. Sick at heart, he set course for Cherbourg. As a forlorn hope, he radioed the map reference of the place where Brandtner had gone down to air-sea rescue.

Ten minutes later, Richter touched down at Cherbourg. His fuel-starved engine cut out on final approach and he just made it over the airfield boundary, his undercarriage collecting a few twigs from a hedge on the way.

The aircraft rolled to a stop in the middle of the runway. A truck raced up and half a dozen airmen jumped out of it, seizing the fighter and pushing it clear.

One of them came up to the pilot and saluted. 'Want a lift over to the flights, sir?' he asked.

Richter shook his head. 'No, thanks. Just get the re-fuellers over as fast as possible. I want to be on my way.'

He went over to the Messerschmitt and walked slowly

round her, stroking the metal of her wings and fuselage. It was warm. He shivered suddenly, thinking of Brandtner and the cold waters of the Channel.

The grass looked inviting. He stretched out on it, revelling in the sunshine and the silence, his head pillowed on his lifejacket. Thirty seconds later, he was fast asleep.

Chapter Five

YEOMAN THREW HIS KIT ON THE BED AND LOOKED around him appreciatively. 'Not bad,' he said. 'Not bad at all.'

Jim Callender crossed the room and threw open the window. The hut looked out over a large field, with cows grazing placidly. Beyond, the roof of a farmhouse peeped out from behind a barrier of trees.

'Well, at least it's an improvement. The north-east was beginning to get right on my nerves.' He gazed thoughtfully out of the window. 'So this is Tangmere.' He jerked a thumb towards the south, where the waters of the Channel lapped against the coast. 'We're right in the front line, boy. Just a few miles of hogwash between us and all the grim nasties. Now we can really get at 'em.'

'It's a pretty good station, this.' The speaker was the room's third occupant, who was lying the wrong way round on his bed with his feet against the wall. His name was Alex McKenna, and despite his Gaelic name he was a Cockney to his fingertips. He wore a flight sergeant's crown above his stripes.

Yeoman looked at him. 'Have you been here before?' he asked.

McKenna blew a leisurely smoke ring. 'Yeah. In thirty-eight, when I was a gunner. Mind, you've got to get away from the station if you want a bit of life. The pubs round about aren't any great shakes. There's one in the village which is very nice; it's a real old-world place, but it's just about been taken over by the officers.

Chichester's not bad, but I always used to go down to Bognor or Brighton. You couldn't go wrong there, especially at the weekly Widows' Ball.'

'Widows' Ball?' Yeoman queried.

McKenna looked at him in mock contempt. 'Where were you brought up?' He sat up on his bed and ran his fingers through his hair, which was sticking out at all sorts of angles.

'The Widows' Ball,' he explained patiently, 'was held every Thursday night, in a certain pub in Brighton. Thursday, you see, happens to be pay-day in this part of the world. So on Thursday night, every female in Brighton who was on the loose descended on this pub in hope of finding a feller.'

'You mean they were prostitutes for one night in the week?'

McKenna looked shocked. 'Good God, no. We never used to *pay* for it. It was almost the other way round. I practically lived with one old dear for six months. Rampant, she was. Must have been forty-five if she was a day, but what a body! Tawny all over, like a lioness. She used to put screens up in her back garden and sunbathe in the nude. And talk about cook! I never tasted food like it.'

Yeoman looked at him sceptically. 'If you were such a brilliant performer,' he asked, 'why did this happy relationship come to an end?'

McKenna waved a hand airily. 'Oh, well, you know how it is – too much of a good thing, and all that. She was getting a bit too possessive, so I decided to shake her off.'

Callender, who knew the speaker of old, roared. 'What the bloody gigolo means is that her husband came back from sea and caught him on the job, or near enough! Exit one NCO sharpish, via drainpipe, pants in hand!'

Yeoman laughed. 'I'd like to have seen it.' The bony, angular McKenna running for his life and clutching his trousers was something that defied the imagination. Callender noticed his expression and slapped him on the back, grinning. 'I can see you don't believe a word he says, but I assure you that all the lies he tells are true. Come on, let's go and grab something to eat.'

They went out of the hut and strolled towards the sergeants' mess. Callender looked up into the sky, squinting against the noonday sun. 'I'd like to bet the bastards are over in force this afternoon,' he said. 'Let's just hope they get our Spits turned round in time, or we'll be sitting ducks.'

It was Sunday 18 August, and 505 Squadron had been at Tangmere for less than an hour. The squadron they had replaced had taken a bad beating the day before and had immediately been sent north for a rest. 505's arrival had caused some confusion; there were two other fighter squadrons at Tangmere and they had both been in action that morning. The new unit had landed just as the Spitfires were being refuelled and rearmed, and had been unceremoniously pushed into a corner of the airfield until the ground crews were free to attend to it. Wing Commander Hillier, on learning that it would be some time before his Spitfires were combat-ready, had at once sent off his pilots to find their accommodation.

There had been no let-up in the German air attacks since the terrific air battles of the fifteenth. When the last enemy bombers droned away across the Channel at the close of that fateful day, they left behind the shattered, burnt-out wrecks of seventy-five of their number scattered over the English countryside. It had been a clear victory for Fighter Command, but a victory bought at a cost of thirty-four Spitfires and Hurricanes.

Tangmere, the most westerly of Number Eleven Group's sector stations, had been badly hit the following day. A force of dive-bombers had struck at the airfield just as the resident fighter squadrons were landing after a sortie. Yeoman and the other newcomers had been appalled at the scene of devastation that greeted them as they taxied their Spitfires across the grass after landing; hangars, workshops, stores, flight huts were all wrecked, and there were craters all over the place. Most of the other buildings on and around the field were damaged to a greater or lesser extent; the officers' and sergeants' messes and their adjacent accommodation seemed to be the only structures that were still completely intact.

The situation on 18 August was gloomy. Already, on this Sunday morning, the Luftwaffe had struck hard at the vital sector stations of Kenley and Biggin Hill, severely damaging the former's all-important operations room. Pilots returning to Tangmere after action told of fierce air battles with superior numbers of Messerschmitt 109s. Yeoman watched them covertly as they sat at the mess tables in their sweat-soaked uniforms, gulping down their food before dashing off to dispersals again. Some, their eyes dull with fatigue, pushed away their plates with the food on them untouched and wandered off in morose silence. Yeoman recognized the symptoms, for he had experienced them himself during three weeks of fighting in France. These were young men whose nerves were as taut as bowstrings; men perilously close to total exhaustion.

Yeoman and his colleagues were halfway through their lunch when Simon Wynne-Williams burst into the room like a cannonball and yelled: '505 to readiness!' They jumped up, scattering knives and forks, and rushed outside, grabbing the nearest bicycles from the rack next to the mess.

'What's going on?' Yeoman shouted, as he pedalled furiously alongside Wynne-Williams.

'There's a big plot building up over the French coast,' the other yelled back. 'We're to go to cockpit readiness. It looks like all hell's going to break loose.'

They reached dispersal and threw their bicycles aside. Most of the other 505 Squadron pilots were already there, strapped into their cockpits. Yeoman climbed on to the port wing of his Spitfire and eased himself into the cockpit, taking care not to ruck the parachute back straps as he did so. They could be very uncomfortable. He strapped on his parachute first: body belt, left shoulder, right shoulder, leg straps through the crutch loop, clicking the metal tags into the quick release box and pulling the harness tight. Then, over the top of the parachute harness, he fastened his safety straps; left shoulder first, then leg straps, then right shoulder. Safety pin slammed into position.

Out of the corner of his eye he saw an airman jump on to the wing of Hillier's aircraft, shout something at the pilot and then jump down again. Hurriedly, Yeoman lifted his helmet from its resting place on the control column and put it on. Hillier raised his arm, giving the signal to start up. Mechanically, Yeoman went through the motions. On either side of him, eleven other pilots were doing the same. Unscrew the Kigass and pump twice to prime the engine; switches on. A nod to the airman standing by with the trolley-acc. Yeoman pressed the starter button and the big propeller began to turn, slowly and unwillingly at first. Then there was the usual cough, a cloud of smoke, and the Merlin blared into life, rumbling and vibrating.

Yeoman set the throttle to a thousand revs, locked the brake lever on the control column and checked the pressures by applying first left and then right rudder. Making sure that the radiator was fully open – otherwise the engine would boil very quickly – he waved his hand from side to side, pulling the cockpit flap closed as his fitter and rigger unplugged the trolley-acc and pulled away the chocks.

He clipped his face mask into place – his cheeks were already clammy with sweat from his exertions and the soft kid of the mask clung to his face uncomfortably – and pressed button A, glancing round at his two wingmen as

54

he did so. Keenan gave him the thumbs-up and the other pilot, a flight sergeant named Honeywell, raised an index finger and thumb joined in a circle. Yeoman grinned behind his mask. He liked Honeywell, a broad, cheerful New Zealander. He hoped the man would enjoy better fortune than Hamilton, lost on his first sortie.

The radio hissed and crackled with atmospherics. Through it all, distorted and tinny, came the voice of the controller: 'Hello, Stingray, Red Box calling, scramble, scramble. Portsmouth, Angels Sixteen.'

Hillier acknowledged and a moment later his Spitfire began to move, followed by the other two fighters of Red Section. Their tails came up and they took off across wind in a cloud of dust and bits of whirling grass. Yellow Section followed suit, and then it was the turn of Yeoman's Blue Section. He trimmed rudder and elevators, checked petrol on and propeller in fine pitch. Mixture rich, and a quick scan of the instruments; oil pressure and glycol temperature both okay.

He opened the throttle to plus two boost and the Spitfire began to roll forward. He eased the stick forward, holding on a little left aileron to counteract the crosswind, then pulled it gently back. The pounding of the undercarriage died away to a dull rumble and then ceased. He was airborne. All around him fighters were lifting away from the ground. He squeezed the brake lever to lock the wheels, then selected undercarriage up. He felt two distinct thumps and the indicator lights winked red at him. He reached up and pulled the hood shut, then closed the radiator flap.

'Hello, Red Box, Stingray calling, all sections airborne.'

'Roger, Stingray. Hello, Red Two, Red Box calling, stand by for pipsqueak zero in fifteen seconds.'

At the right-hand side of each Spitfire's cockpit there was a little pointer and a dial marked off in four fifteen-second sections. This piece of equipment, when switched on, sent out a high-pitched fifteen-second transmission to the ground station, enabling the latter to tune in and fix the position of each section, advising details of its whereabouts to the operations rooms controlling the fighter formations. Transmitting for a fix in this way was the job of the number two aircraft in each section. Yeoman heard the ground station call up each one in turn:

'. . . five, four, three, two, one, zero . . . pip in, Blue Two, pip in.'

The high-pitched squawk momentarily drowned all other radio noise as Keenan pressed down the switch. 'Hello, Red Box, Blue Two calling, pip in, pip in, listening out.'

The twelve Spitfires pointed their noses into the blue vault of the sky, climbing steadily at two thousand feet per minute. Adrenalin pumped through twelve bodies as the pilots began their endless, life-preserving search of the sky around them; left, right, above, below, behind, into the hostile sun.

'Hello, Stingray, Red Box calling, vector 250.'

The formation turned, heading west-south-west. At ten thousand feet, Yeoman turned on his oxygen, then as an afterthought turned it off again. He would wait until he reached fifteen thousand feet before turning it on again. Pilots had been lost because their oxygen ran out during a dogfight at high level.

The Channel was over on the left, shimmering and glassy under the sun. The Isle of Wight showed up darkly, like a great ink stain. From time to time, Yeoman dropped his eyes from the sky search to scan his instruments, instantly correcting any tendency of the Merlin to use too much power. Everything was vital; the avoidance of excessive throttle movements or an over-rich mixture became of paramount importance, points that could save precious fuel for use in an emergency.

'Hello Stingray, Red Box calling, sixty plus bandits in your nine o'clock.'

Twelve pairs of eyes turned seawards, narrowing against the brassy glare reflected from the surface of the water. There was a moment's pause, then Hillier radioed: 'I haven't got 'em. What are they doing?'

'They're going across into your ten o'clock. Closing fast.'

Suddenly, the R/T echoed with a wild shout from Red Three. 'I see 'em! Ten o'clock low. Christ, they're Stukas!'

'Okay, I've got 'em now.' A pause, then: 'No fighter escort. Bloody hell, no fighter escort! All sections, attack, attack!'

Yeoman turned the knurled knob on top of the stick from 'safe' to 'fire' and switched on his reflector sight. Oxygen on full, mixture lever to fully rich, throttle open slightly. The whole enemy formation was clearly visible now, six waves of Stuka dive-bombers flying ten abreast. They must be bloody mad, Yeoman thought, venturing over here without fighter protection. It was the Spitfire pilot's dream. He recalled the punishment the Stukas had taken over Calais and Dunkirk a few months earlier.

The Spitfires dived on the Stukas like a school of sharks, curving down to attack from astern. It was ridiculously easy, almost like an air firing practice. Yeoman's section went after half a dozen Stukas that suddenly broke away and went into a shallow dive. They seemed to be heading for the airfield of Thorney Island. Yeoman centred one gull-winged shape in his reflector sight and closed in, ignoring the tracer that zipped past him from the rear gun. He opened fire at 150 yards and kept on firing, chopping the Stuka to pieces with short, deadly bursts. At a hundred yards the rear gunner stopped firing; at fifty yards the Stuka began to burn, flames pouring back along its fuselage. Yeoman pulled aside hastily as his target lost speed and dropped away, tumbling over and over.

Stukas were going down in flames on all sides. A second RAF fighter squadron had arrived and hurled itself into the fray, filling the R/T with shouts and whoops of jubilation. Yeoman could not help but admire the bravery of the German pilots; despite their terrible losses, they closed the gaps in their ranks and pressed on.

Suddenly, Yeoman heard the urgent voice of Simon Wynne-Williams over the radio. 'Stingray aircraft, this is Stingray Green One. Look out, fighters coming down hard from seven o'clock!'

Yeoman craned his neck. Sure enough, there they were, a great number of twin-engined Messerschmitt 110s, falling out of the eastern sky. They were the Stukas' escort, but they had arrived too late to save a score of the luckless bombers.

Simon Wynne-Williams, who had been the first to spot the threat in the excitement of the chase, turned his Green Section away from the Stukas they had been harrying and went for the 110s head-on. Disjointed voices continued to crackle over the radio as more enemy fighters appeared, single-engined Messerschmitt 109s this time. It was difficult to work out who was calling whom, especially when pilots forgot to give call-signs in the heat of the moment.

'Thirty plus, going from two to three o'clock.'

'Okay Jock, we're looking. No contact yet.'

'They're passing from three to four o'clock now, parallel. No panic yet.'

'Roger, okay, okay, I see 'em now.'

'Greyhound Red Section, look out below.'

'109s behind, watch it.'

'Aircraft four o'clock, climbing.'

'Greyhound leader to all sections, close up. Turning starboard.'

Who the hell was Greyhound? Yeoman wondered, as he brought his own section round to help Wynne-Williams take on the 110s. Then he heard Hillier's voice, calm and reassuring.

'Stingray leader to Stingray Yellow Section, 109s above you and behind. Coming down on you now.'

'Roger, leader, I can't see the bastards. Tell me when to break.'

'Hold it, hold it . . . break!'

'Get stuck in, everybody.'

'Yellow Two, break right!'

'Christ, that was close!'

The voices were taut now, charged with the strain of air combat, of handling the speed-stiffened controls of fighters cleaving through the sky at 350 miles an hour.

'Stingray Red Section, there's half a dozen of the buggers right on top of you.'

'For Christ's sake get a move on, Red Three!'

'Get your own bloody finger out, that bastard nearly had me then!'

'It's okay, I'm watching your tail.'

'Yellow One calling, can't see a bloody thing . . . oil everywhere.'

'Get the hell out of it, then.' Yeoman grinned, recognizing Jim Callender's drawl. The lanky American's philosophy was simple; if you found yourself with the slightest problem in the middle of a fight, stick your nose down and run like hell. You stayed alive, that way.

Wynne-Williams' section, up on top of the scrap, had come into brutal contact with the leading 110s. Two of them were already going down, staining the sky with smoke. A Spitfire tried to limp away, streaming a white trail of glycol, only to be pounced on by two 109s. With horrible finality, it rolled slowly over on its back and its nose went down until it was diving vertically. A few thousand feet lower down, it exploded. There was no parachute.

Wynne-Williams closed in on a 110, setting its port engine on fire. He saw the observer struggle clear and bale out, but the pilot remained at the controls and turned seawards in a gallant attempt to escape. Wynne-Williams followed, getting into position to deliver the *coup de grâce*.

59

His thumb caressed the gun-button, but he never fired. In that instant, the world blew up in his face. A cannon shell exploded under his seat, sending white-hot splinters searing into the backs of both legs. A second shattered his cockpit canopy and tore his scalp to shreds under his leather helmet; and a third, the most damaging of all, slammed into the upper fuel tank on the other side of the instrument panel.

Instantly, the Spitfire's cockpit became a roaring inferno. Semi-conscious and blinded with blood from his scalp wounds, the pilot clawed at his safety harness, ready to fling himself over the side, away from the blistering flames.

Then, through the fog of pain and smoke, something shot into sudden focus ahead of him. It was a Messerschmitt 109, presumably his attacker. A blind, all-consuming rage and hatred filled him and he hurled his Spitfire in pursuit, tucking up his feet to escape the worst of the flames. He wore no flying boots, and his trouser legs were burning. The 109's wings filled his sights and he pressed the gun-button. His eight guns roared; one burst was enough. The 109's tail flew apart and the remainder flicked into a series of fast rolls, disappearing below and behind.

Through the red film that covered his eyes, Wynne-Williams looked down at the hands that gripped the control column and throttle lever. His fingers looked like blackened bananas, with the skin cracking and peeling away. In front of him, the instrument panel seemed to flow before his eyes. He shook his head to dispel the illusion, then realized dimly that it was no illusion after all; the panel was melting in the intense heat.

Somehow, he tore his hands free and reached up, tugging at the cockpit canopy. It slid back easily and he breathed a prayer of thanks for his ground crew, whose attentions had ensured its smooth function.

Flames burgeoned around him as air rushed into the cockpit. The skin of his face was burning. He gripped the edge of the cockpit and cried out in agony as the metal bit cruelly into the charred flesh of his palms. Clenching his teeth, he levered himself head-first over the side. The slipstream caught him and whirled him away from the stricken fighter.

He left a streamer of smoke behind him as he fell, his body wreathed in flames. His fingers groped desperately for the D-ring. They were swollen and locked stiffly, and it was several agonizing seconds before he was able to grasp it firmly. He pulled hard, nearly passing out with the pain.

His parachute opened with a crack and a jerk that almost tore his tortured body in half. Gasping for breath, he beat at his smouldering clothing. Already, the blood on his face was congealing into a hard mask. He forced one swollen eyelid open and looked down. He was drifting over open countryside, mercifully clear of woodland. Unable to control his descent properly, he would have to take his chance on landing.

The air rushed past him, turning the exposed areas of his flayed skin into deep pools of pain. He was falling too quickly. His parachute canopy was full of splinter holes; the seat pack must have saved his life.

There was nothing he could do except wait for the impact. His mind functioned with a strange clarity; he felt an odd sense of peace. He was going to die, and there was no point in making a fuss about it. Better to go this way, anyhow, than to linger on for the rest of his life as a scarred travesty of a human being.

He never saw the ground race up to meet him. He was totally blind now, his seared eyelids gummed shut. He slammed feet-first through a tall hedge and into a ditch. The impact knocked him unconscious instantly. He lay there face down in mud and watery slime, like a blackened log. The hot buckles of his parachute harness made a faint hissing noise, and a wisp of steam curled among the undergrowth.

Two and a half miles above, a desperate air battle flared across the sky. Beneath it, the surviving Stukas slipped away across the Channel. They would not be coming back. The much-vaunted dive-bomber had made its last appearance in English skies.

Yeoman had seen Wynne-Williams go down in flames, but there had been no time to investigate his friend's fate. Within seconds, he had found himself fighting for his own life as his section became entangled in a whirling mass of Messerschmitt 109s and 110s. His Spitfire shuddered as a cannon shell slammed into it somewhere behind the cockpit, and the fighter went into a spin without warning. He regained control and pulled out of the spin four thousand feet lower down. He looked round in time to see a pair of 109s diving hard at him; there was no sign of any friendly aircraft.

He was hopelessly trapped. Another cannon shell punched a hole in his port wing root and something kicked his left foot hard. He experienced an odd sensation, like pins and needles, but felt no pain.

The two 109s were harassing him, edging him towards the coast. He knew that with his aircraft damaged, he was no match for the pair of them. Deliberately, he pulled back the stick and closed the throttle, putting on hard right rudder as the fighter lost airspeed. An instant later, the Spitfire went over into another spin.

These tactics had got him out of a jam once before, over France, and he prayed fervently that they would work on this occasion. He held the fighter in the spin, watching the earth rotate around him in a brown-green blur. The altimeter unwound with frightening speed, the needle sweeping away the thousands of feet.

At five thousand feet he eased off the pressure on the stick and pushed forward his left leg to apply opposite rudder.

The leg refused to move. There was no feeling at all below the knee. He tried again, mouth gaping with the effort, willing his muscles to obey the frantic commands of his brain. This time, a violent pain stabbed through his whole leg, tearing at his groin. He cried out involuntarily but gritted his teeth and kept up the pressure, realizing that the pain must mean that his left foot was pushing against the rudder pedal.

The dizzy rotation slowed and then stopped altogether. The Spitfire plunged earthwards in a steep dive. Yeoman gripped the stick with both hands and pulled with all his strength. The aircraft responded unwillingly, its nose coming up inch by inch towards the horizon.

A bulbous silvery object flashed past, followed by another and another. Yeoman's heart almost stopped. He was streaking at nearly four hundred miles per hour through the middle of the Portsmouth balloon barrage. Flak burst around him as trigger-happy gunners opened up. A cable flashed past his wingtip, missing his speeding aircraft by inches.

He opened the throttle and pulled back the stick, sending the fighter bounding into the air. The 'g' pressed him down into his seat and he blacked out, regaining his senses seconds later to find the instrument panel swimming in front of his eyes. The Spitfire was in a near-vertical climb at full throttle, already passing through six thousand feet. The Portsmouth anti-aircraft gunners were still doing their best to shoot him down. It was high time to get out of it.

He levelled out and put the Spitfire into a shallow dive, turning eastwards in the direction of Tangmere. His aircraft was vibrating badly, but the engine was running smoothly enough and he knew that if she didn't catch fire she would see him home. His leg and foot were his main worry; the pain was hitting him with a vengeance now, rolling through him in waves like savage toothache. Some sensation had returned to his toes; they felt sticky, but

63

whether with sweat or blood he had no means of knowing. Probably both.

He stayed low down during the short flight back to base, scanning the sky constantly. Apart from a flight of Hurricanes, a few thousand feet higher and heading west, he saw no other aircraft.

His radio was still working and he called up Tangmere, asking for and getting permission to 'pancake'. Landing was tricky; he felt light-headed and his hands trembled, making it hard for him to set up a steady approach. He could have almost wept with relief when the undercarriage came down; he felt he no longer had the strength to cope with a belly landing. Still, it was difficult enough. His flaps refused to work and he touched down at fairly high speed, bounding across the airfield in a series of kangaroo leaps before the fighter settled at last. He taxied to dispersal, streaming sweat, the pain in his foot growing worse every minute.

He managed to unfasten his straps and then slumped in his seat, exhausted. His fitter, LAC Morton, jumped on the wing, took one look at Yeoman's pale, drawn face, and at once yelled for help.

'Two-six over here, quick! The pilot's hurt!' He turned back to Yeoman, his face concerned. 'Where did they get you, Sarge? Your kite's taken a bit of a beating.'

Yeoman managed a weak grin. 'Okay, Jack, don't panic. Just a splinter or two in the foot, that's all. Got myself a Stuka.'

Morton's face lit up. 'Good-oh! The squadron's really gone to town today. Hang on, we'll have you out of there in a jiff. Here's the blood wagon.'

An ambulance rolled up, and an airman jumped on the other wing of the Spitfire. Yeoman hooked an arm round his neck and the other round Morton's, and between them they eased him out of the cockpit. As they did so, the pilot caught sight of his left foot and winced. His shoe – he seldom flew in flying boots because of the heat, preferring to tuck his trouser bottoms into his socks, like a cyclist – was in ribbons. Blood oozed darkly through the holes; the whole cockpit floor was covered in it. Sudden panic gripped him. God, he thought, what if they have to take it off? He pushed the thought aside, swallowing hard.

They laid him out on a stretcher and he cried out involuntarily as a spasm of white-hot pain lanced through his foot. Someone gave him a shot of morphine. His last impression, before he passed out, was of the ambulance doors slamming, shutting out the sun.

'So, you've woken up at last.'

Yeoman moved his head groggily and a face swam into focus. It grinned at him. He recognized Squadron Leader McKenzie, the senior medical officer. For a second or two, Yeoman wondered where he was. Then, remembering, he tried to sit up, opening his mouth to speak. His throat was dry and parched and only a croak came out.

McKenzie pushed him back on to the pillow. 'It's all right. Take it easy. Your foot's still in one piece, although we pulled enough scrap iron out of it to build a tank. Want a look?'

Yeoman nodded and McKenzie reached for a small tray on the bedside locker. On it lay half a dozen pieces of rusty-looking metal, the size of a thumb nail or less. They had jagged edges. Yeoman suddenly felt sick.

McKenzie laughed. 'I thought you'd like them,' he said. 'You can have 'em for a souvenir, if you want. Here, drink this.'

He handed Yeoman a glass full of pinkish liquid. The pilot eyed it dubiously. 'Go on,' the MO urged, 'take it. It'll do you good. It's my universal remedy for all ills, from bullet holes to pimples on the bum.'

Yeoman drank, and began to feel better almost at once. He looked down the bed. His foot was propped up, tightly swathed in bandages up to the ankle. He looked at McKenzie.

'Is it going to be okay?' he asked.

'Oh, sure. Don't worry about it. I've seen worse injuries as a result of mess parties. Mind you, you'll be laid up for a while. It'll be a good three weeks before you're in a fit state to do any more flying, although you can be up and about inside a week, if you're a good lad and do as you're told. I daresay we can find things for you to do. Now, I suggest you make the most of it and get some rest. One of the orderlies will be round with some food later on.'

Yeoman settled back against the pillow and plucked idly at the bedclothes. He still felt drugged, and his thoughts wandered. Above all, he hated the idea of being confined to bed, a useless liability, at this critical time. It was going to be hard to endure.

He drifted off to sleep. It was dusk when he awoke. His door was ajar and a naked electric light bulb glowed dimly in the corridor outside. He wondered, for the first time, what building he was in; it couldn't be sick quarters, because that had been pulverized by an enemy bomb.

The door was pushed wide open and an orderly came in, carrying a tray. On it was a plate of sausage and mash and a mug of tea. Yeoman suddenly felt ravenously hungry. The orderly placed the tray on the locker, crossed the room and pulled the heavy curtains, then switched on the light.

'Evenin',' he said, turning to the pilot. 'Thought you were never goin' to wake up.'

He helped Yeoman to sit up in bed and placed the tray across his thighs. Yeoman grunted as his foot throbbed, and eased it into a more comfortable position.

'Hurt, does it?' the orderly enquired cheerfully. 'Never mind, Sarge, soon be up and about again. Privileged, that's what you are. Know what this place is? Part of the officers' mess, that's what. You won't be lording it all on your own for long, though. We're moving a couple of other blokes in here later on. Poles, they are. Mad buggers. Really good company, if you 'appen to speak Polish. By the way, you've got a visitor.'

The visitor was Jim Callender. Yeoman felt a great upsurge of friendship as he breezed into the room. The American looked dog-tired, but his grin was bright enough. He grabbed a sausage from Yeoman's plate and bit into it.

'Well, George,' he said, chewing furiously, 'what's the verdict?'

Yeoman told him what the MO had said, and asked how the squadron had fared during the afternoon's air battle. Callender slammed his clenched fist into the open palm of his other hand.

'We really clobbered 'em,' he said. 'The Huns lost thirty Stukas all told, and we got twelve of 'em – not to mention a couple of 110s and a 109. We lost three kites, though, and most of the others are damaged. Between you and me, I don't think we can stand the pace for much longer, especially if they keep on hitting the airfields. We're knocking a hell of a lot of them down, but if they can keep up this kind of pace we're going to run out of fighters and pilots in about ten days, by my reckoning. Pilots, most of all. Some of the squadrons have really taken a beating.'

It was a sobering thought. Suddenly, Yeoman remembered Wynne-Williams.

'What happened to Simon?' he asked. 'I saw him going down.'

Callender hesitated for a moment. Then he said: 'He baled out.'

Yeoman felt a vast relief. 'Thank God for that, at least,' he said. 'That's really good news.'

Callender's face was serious, his eyes haunted by an expression Yeoman couldn't quite place.

'Not really,' he said quietly. 'You see, he burned. He hasn't got a face any more.'

Chapter Six

YEOMAN POPPED LIKE A CORK FROM THE GATE OF platform three, pressured by the crush of people behind him, and stood helplessly in the main concourse of Waterloo Station. The great mass of the crowd flowed around him, moving this way and that. He spotted a news-stand, an island of refuge in the human sea, and forced his way towards it, leaning heavily on his stick. A railway porter took him by the arm, helping him along.

'Come on there,' the man called, 'make a bit of room. Can't you see the lad's wounded?'

Yeoman reached the news-stand, feeling somewhat embarrassed, and thanked the porter. The man touched his cap in a friendly gesture and moved away.

Someone rose from a nearby seat and the pilot sank gratefully into the vacant space. He'd had about enough for one morning. The journey from the south coast had seemed endless, the train stopping every couple of miles, and the bombastic conversation of his fellow-travellers had put him in a foul mood. They were businessmen from the City, and one of them – a florid-faced, whisky-soaked individual with a plummy voice – had spent the entire trip complaining about shortages. Yeoman had been on the point of ramming his stick down the man's throat when, mercifully, the train had reached London.

Squadron Leader McKenzie was right, Yeoman reflected. If anything, the MO had been over-optimistic. It was nearly three weeks now since he had been wounded, and his foot still hadn't healed properly. Still, he felt confident that he could handle a Spitfire – and the way things were going he was sure that he would not be kept on the ground much longer, even with a damaged foot.

Bad weather on 19 August had brought the RAF a much-needed respite, but even so the depleted fighter squadrons were in a bad way when the attacks resumed in earnest on the twenty-third. During the last week of August the Luftwaffe had really stepped up its assault, hammering again and again at the RAF airfields that lay in a defensive half-circle before London: Kenley, Redhill, Biggin Hill, West Malling, Detling and Gravesend to the south-east; Hornchurch, Rochford, Debden and North Weald to the north-east. On the thirtieth Biggin Hill had been completely wrecked by a squadron of low-flying Dorniers, attacking with 1,000-pound bombs, and a lot of valuable personnel had been killed or wounded. Fortunately, the station's two Spitfire squadrons had been airborne at the time.

Other airfields had been hit equally badly, if not worse. Manston, the Kentish airfield from which Yeoman had helped to cover the Dunkirk evacuation in May, had been completely abandoned, its surface pitted and cratered like the face of the moon. Hornchurch had also been badly hit, and here the squadrons had not been so lucky; the base had been attacked just as a squadron of Spitfires was taking off, and several had been destroyed. The last day of August, in particular, had been a bad one for Fighter Command; thirty-nine enemy aircraft had been shot down, but thirty-two Spitfires and Hurricanes had been destroyed too.

Yeoman had been allowed out of bed after a week and, equipped with a pair of crutches and later a stick, was assigned to the operations room at Tangmere. From his position on the raised dais with its bank of telephones at the fighter controller's elbow, he had participated in the daily battles at second hand, following the movement of the coloured counters on the plotting table below and listening for the profane shouts over the loudspeaker that were the war cries of young men locked in mortal combat miles above the earth. Yeoman had found his days in the operations room intensely dramatic and charged with suspense; more so, in some ways, than if he had been fighting in the cockpit of his Spitfire.

Yes, a great deal had happened during the past three weeks. For a start, the Luftwaffe had bombed London on 25 August. Some said it had been a mistake, that the Germans had been going for oil storage tanks up the river – a legitimate military target – but whatever the truth RAF Bomber Command had attacked Berlin the next night by way of reprisal. The gloves were off with a vengeance now, and the ordeal of the cities was beginning.

Yeoman got up and limped over to the news-stand. He bought a paper and turned to his seat again, only to find that it had been occupied by an enormously fat woman. She glared at him belligerently, as though daring him to challenge her. He smiled at her and winked, leaned against the wooden side of the kiosk, and opened his paper.

He scanned the news headlines briefly, smiling to himself at their greatly inflated optimism. According to the headlines, Fighter Command was winning the battle by a handsome margin. Still, that was what the public wanted to hear. Britain was a frightened, uncertain nation, still shaken by the hammer-blows her forces had sustained on the Continent and in Norway, and it would not take much to destroy civilian morale. Anyway, the people seemed to accept the inflated figures of enemy aircraft destroyed without question; the pilots, however, knew differently. It always happened in the heat of air combat; three or four pilots would fire at one bomber, and if it went down they would all claim it as their own 'kill'.

The true facts were infinitely more alarming. On the

first day of September, according to the reports of RAF fighter pilots, the Germans had begun to tighten up their escort procedures. The ratio now was roughly four fighters to every bomber. One strong German formation had bombed the docks at Tilbury unmolested simply because Fighter Command had not been able to break through the screen of Messerschmitts.

One thing puzzled Yeoman. No doubt it was puzzling the air staff even more. Suddenly, at a point when Fighter Command seemed about to fall apart at the seams, the Germans had cut down their attacks on the British fighter airfields and focused their attention on London. Smoke was still rising from the London docks, which had been heavily attacked on the night of 5 September. Now, two days later, London was a nervous city, wondering when the raiders would come again.

He folded the paper and tossed it into a waste-paper bin. He looked at his watch; it was twelve-thirty. He felt a sudden twinge of alarm. Julia was late; suppose she had missed him in the crowd and gone away again? All kinds of thoughts flashed through his mind. He turned his head this way and that, searching frantically for a glimpse of her.

'Hello, George.' The voice came softly at his elbow.

He turned. She was not as he remembered her. Her red hair was cropped short and tucked under a small cap. She wore a grey nurse's uniform. Her green eyes regarded him steadily, and there were dark shadows of weariness under them.

Suddenly, the green eyes filled with tears. 'Oh, George,' she said, 'you're hurt. Why didn't you tell me?'

Her left hand came up and touched him gently on the cheek. Awkwardly, leaning on his stick, he put his own free hand around her waist and pulled her towards him, kissing her on the forehead. Her arms went about his neck and she clung to him tightly. He could feel her trembling slightly through the roughness of his uniform.

'It's all right, love,' he told her. 'Just a scratch, really. It'll be okay in a day or two.'

She pulled away from him a little and looked up into his face, her nose red. She sniffled and managed a watery smile, then, rummaging in her shoulder bag, she produced a handkerchief and blew her nose.

'Sorry, George. It's just – well, it's just that I'm so glad to see you in one piece. It's been such a long time.'

He smiled and took the handkerchief from her, gently wiping away a tear that trickled down the side of her nose. 'I never realized I had this kind of effect on women,' he said jokingly.

'Oh, it's not just you. I'm worn out, George. I've just come off duty, you know. I'm a VAD, now. Doing my bit for the Old Country.'

'You're a what?' he asked.

'VAD stands for Voluntary Aid Detachment. We're auxiliary nurses. Come on, let's go and find a restaurant and I'll treat you to some lunch. We've a lot to talk about.'

They took the Underground from Waterloo to Blackfriars, emerging into the early afternoon sunshine. Arm in arm, they walked through the heartland of Britain's newspaper industry into Fleet Street. Yeoman was fascinated; he had worked for a time on a newspaper in Yorkshire before the war, and he had always wanted to visit Fleet Street. Now he was here at last, but under far different circumstances from any he had ever envisaged.

Julia led him to a pub which was famous for its associations with Charles Dickens and a host of other well-known writers since his day. The dining room was crowded, but Julia was evidently a regular customer and they were quickly shown to a vacant table for two.

She grinned at Yeoman as they sat down. 'Being heavily involved in the newspaper world has its compensations,' she said. 'Now, are you going to let me organize you and trust my excellent judgment, or will your masculine pride be hurt if I order?'

Yeoman laughed. 'You go right ahead,' he told her. 'You organized me pretty well in France, if you remember, and when it comes to food I haven't got any pride. I could eat a horse.'

The lunch – traditionally English, with oxtail soup followed by roast beef with Yorkshire pudding and vegetables, then apple pie and cream – was excellent. Yeoman had tasted nothing like it since before the war. It was clear that, even in wartime, Fleet Street looked after its own.

Julia was ravenous too, and there was little conversation during the meal. Afterwards, satisfied, they settled down over a cup of tea – no coffee was available – and appraised one another. Yeoman lit his pipe, which made Julia laugh.

'I see you've acquired the odd anti-social habit since I saw you last,' she said. 'That puts me one up on you. I seem to remember I once offered you a cigarette and you looked at me as though I'd made an immoral suggestion. I stopped smoking weeks ago.'

'I'm very glad to hear it,' the pilot retorted. 'I think it's highly un-feminine. But then, I'm old-fashioned. Have you noticed the way I've been looking at you?'

She looked at him archly. 'It hasn't escaped my attention, but we'll have none of that in here – this is a respectable pub. There's a time and place for everything.'

He took her hand in his and squeezed it. 'You said we had a lot to talk about,' he said. 'You first. I want to know all your adventures since you got out of France. How did you come to be mixed up with the VADs, or whatever you call them?'

She looked at him seriously. 'There were two reasons, mainly. The first, of course, is that I'm a journalist first and foremost, and I wanted to put some really accurate stuff in front of the people back home. You can't do that second-hand. You've got to get involved.'

There was a strange expression on her face, a mixture

of determination and earnestness that gave her a kind of beauty Yeoman had not seen before. 'That wasn't the principal reason, though,' she went on. 'George, this is my fight, too. It has been ever since we were in France, and I saw what was happening to ordinary, innocent people.'

She looked down suddenly and her voice grew very quiet and full of emotion. 'I was down at the docks the night before last,' she said. 'There was a church in one of the streets . . . people, women and children mostly, were sheltering there when the bombers came. They were in a vault underneath the building. A bomb came through the wall of the church, went straight through the floor and exploded among them.'

Her voice shook. 'It was hideous . . . unimaginable. Bodies . . . limbs and bits of flesh, all mixed up with clothing and children's toys. People were literally blown to pieces.

'We got there a few minutes after the bomb fell. The raid was still in progress and there were explosions and fires all around. I was terrified; we all were. We had a hard time getting into the vault, because the only entrance was choked with bodies. The bomb had set fire to a big pile of coke, too, and we could hardly see.'

She choked suddenly, her whole body shaking. 'What we saw in there was bad enough, but that wasn't the worst. The ARP men brought the bodies out, and . . . and we had to help piece them together ready for burial.'

She gripped his arm tightly and turned an anguished face towards him. 'Oh, George, it was just like a horrible jigsaw puzzle, with a lot of the bits missing. We worked in pairs, a few minutes at a time, because we couldn't stand it any longer than that. I'll never forget the awful smell as long as I live – that, and the knowledge that these frightful lumps of flesh had once been living, breathing people, made it an utter nightmare.

'Maybe I coped better than some of the others because

74

I'd studied anatomy at college, and I tried to imagine I was back in the anatomy class again. But nothing seemed to fit. We would put one body together, only to find that a lot of bits were missing from another. We just kept being sick all the time.' She buried her face in her hands, sobbing. Yeoman put his arm round her shoulders and held her close. People were staring at them curiously.

'Come on, love,' he said, 'let's get out of here.'

She patted his hand. 'I'm sorry about all this, George,' she apologized, 'but I've been bottling it up inside me for nearly two days now. You've no idea what a relief it is just to talk about it. I was on duty until ten this morning, too, so I'm just about all-in. Would you mind very much if we just went home?'

He told her he did not, and they went out into the street. Suddenly, she stopped dead and turned to him.

'I've been going on about my own troubles so much you haven't had a chance to get a word in, poor dear. I haven't even asked you how long you've got before you have to go back.'

Yeoman smiled. 'Forty-eight hours,' he told her. He patted the gas-mask container slung over his shoulder in regulation style. 'Brought my toothbrush and pyjamas, just in case I happen to meet an obliging young lady.'

She laughed at him. 'You're a tonic. All I want right now is sleep. We can talk about the pyjamas later.'

Together, they walked towards the Underground. Around them, the sirens were wailing.

Her flat was in Kensington, on the second floor of one of those faceless but solidly imposing Victorian houses that characterized the London suburbs. She shared it with a telephone supervisor who worked at the US Embassy, a girl called Sheila, but Sheila was away on leave and Julia and Yeoman had the place to themselves.

Julia, so tired that she had barely been able to manage the stairs, had collapsed on her bed fully clothed and fallen into a deep sleep almost at once. Yeoman had taken a bath and shaved, then settled down in the small lounge to read and wait for her to come round.

He must have dozed for a while, too. The noise of the sirens roused him and he looked at his watch; it was nearly six o'clock. He peeped into the bedroom; Julia was nowhere to be seen, but he could hear water running in the bathroom.

He crossed the lounge. French windows opened on to a small balcony and he stepped outside, looking up into the eastern sky. It was criss-crossed from horizon to horizon by innumerable vapour trails. As he watched, the first sticks of bombs went down into the East End, exploding with a roar that made London tremble. Leisurely, great mushrooms of black and brown smoke, boiling with crimson at their heart, climbed into the rays of the evening sun. There was no wind and they hung there, expanding very slowly, feeding on the fires at their roots. More explosions boomed out, making the windows around Yeoman rattle alarmingly, and more evil, cancerous pillars erected themselves. A slate, loosened by the concussions, rattled down a nearby roof and shattered on the pavement below.

He caught a whiff of perfume, and half turned. Julia was standing at his elbow, her eyes wide.

'It's horrifying,' she said. 'Horrifying, but there's a kind of beauty in it. A strange, violent beauty.' She pointed. 'Look . . . those thin trails up there. Are those our fighters?'

Yeoman nodded. The air battle that was raging three miles above the London docks was too distant for him to make out any details, although a gleaming dot showed up now and then as an aircraft turned, catching the sun.

He circled her waist with his arm. She wore a silken dressing gown, and his heart leaped at the firm pressure of her supple body against his hand. Suddenly, she pressed

76

herself tightly against him. He buried his face in her hair. The fragrance of violets filled his nostrils.

'George,' she whispered, 'dear George. It could be you up there. Thank God it isn't. I can't bear the thought of anything happening to you.'

He started to speak, to reassure her, to tell her that he would always be there for her, that he loved her and wanted her and that his heart was bursting with happiness and a kind of pain, all at the same time. He cupped her face in his hands and she placed a finger against his lips.

'Not now, darling,' she said softly. 'Don't say anything now. Just make love to me.'

The bombers returned that night, unloading their cargoes of death into the glowing inferno of the East End. All night long the thunder went on, splitting the sky asunder.

In the whole of tortured London, two people at least took no notice of it.

Chapter Seven

YEOMAN, SURROUNDED BY A CLOUD OF TOBACCO smoke, was allowing himself the luxury of half an hour in the latrine. He was pleased with himself. The latrine was a makeshift affair, a row of canvas cubicles equipped with ashcans, hastily erected near the readiness hut to replace a more permanent structure which had been destroyed in an air raid.

For once, Yeoman had managed to secure the cubicle at the eastern end of the line. It was much in demand early in the morning, for the sun shone through a series of tears in the canvas side, making it quite pleasant to sit there in complete privacy. The noises of the airfield were muted, forming a vague background to Yeoman's reverie. Idly, he contemplated a fly that was sitting in a patch of sunlight, flexing its wings. It moved suddenly, crawling to the edge of the pool of light, then stopped again, as though reluctant to venture on to the darker area of canvas.

Yeoman drew on his pipe and expelled a cloud of smoke towards the insect. It twitched, then took off suddenly and dived, buzzing low over the floor and escaping through the gap under the door.

It was 11 September, and Yeoman had been back with the squadron for two days. He smiled, remembering the reception he had got from his friends; their jibes had pulled him down with a crash from cloud nine, which was just as well. He would soon be in action again, and would need all his mental resources to cope with the demands of combat. Thoughts of Julia, for the time being, would have to be pushed to the back of his mind.

His injured foot still pained him from time to time, but at least he knew now that he could handle a Spitfire without undue discomfort. The MO had reluctantly authorized his return to flying duties on the afternoon of the tenth and he had lost no time in finding himself a spare fighter, taking her up to ten thousand feet and pushing her through the full range of aerobatics. The effort had made him sweat, but he had landed with the comforting knowledge that he had lost none of his skill.

A sudden bellow from outside startled him. 'George! Are you in there?'

Yeoman sighed. 'No,' he said.

The canvas structure swayed alarmingly as someone buffeted it from outside. Yeoman recognized Honeywell's voice. 'Oh, come on,' the New Zealander yelled, 'give your backside a chance! The boss wants to see you.'

Yeoman emerged half a minute later, blinking in the sunlight and fastening his tunic. 'Now what have I done?' he asked. The other shrugged. 'God knows,' he answered, 'but the adj. said it was pretty urgent. I'd get a move on, if I were you. You know Hillier doesn't like to be kept waiting.'

Yeoman walked quickly past the parked Spitfires towards the squadron offices, nodding to the ground crews who called out cheerfully to him. He knew that he was popular, and it made him feel good inside. He was a man who liked to be liked, and was conscious that it was one of his failings.

The squadron offices ran alongside one of the hangars. The main structure had been half demolished, but the offices themselves had escaped undamaged, apart from shattered windows. Yeoman went inside and collided with the adjutant, Flight Lieutenant King, who was making a beeline for the door with a large sheaf of papers under his arm. King, who wore two rows of First World War ribbons under a Royal Flying Corps brevet, grinned at the younger man in friendly fashion.

'Ah, Yeoman,' he said, 'the co is expecting you. Go right in.' He winked. 'And don't look so apprehensive. He's in a good mood.' King nodded benignly and limped off, his artificial leg creaking faintly.

Yeoman took a deep breath and crossed the room, adjusting his forage cap as he went. He knocked on the door of Hillier's office and a crisp voice ordered him to enter.

Wing Commander Richard Fitzhugh Hillier, DFC, AFC, was standing by the window, hands clasped behind his back, gazing out over the airfield. Yeoman stood at attention for long seconds, waiting for his commanding officer to turn round. At last Hillier swivelled to face him, and he saluted. Hillier nodded and crossed to his desk, sitting down heavily. The aristocratic features split in a brief smile, and Yeoman was startled. He had never seen Hillier smile before.

'All right, Yeoman,' he said, 'relax.' The young pilot's feet moved to the 'at ease' position and he winced a little as he felt a sudden twinge of pain. The shadow that crossed his face did not go unnoticed.

'Sit down, Yeoman,' Hillier ordered, indicating a wicker chair. 'Is your foot still troubling you?'

'Just a little, sir, now and again. But I can handle a Spit okay, and the MO seems quite happy,' he added hurriedly.

Hillier grunted. 'All right, I don't need to be convinced.' He looked down at a file that lay open on his desk. 'You've got seven confirmed,' he stated abruptly, 'which puts you in the squadron's top four when it comes to shooting Huns down.' He leaned back and stared hard at the pilot, who fidgeted.

Hillier flashed another of his watery smiles, and continued: 'Remember that bollocking I gave you in France for going off and chasing Huns without proper authorization? Your first day on the squadron, wasn't it?'

'Yes, sir. It wasn't a very good start.'

'Well, no doubt you're experienced enough now to realize the sense behind the reprimand. You've come a long way since then.'

Just what the hell is all this leading up to? Yeoman wondered. Hillier didn't keep him in the dark for long.

'Yeoman,' he said, 'I think it's time you took on more responsibility. How do you feel about it?'

In for a penny, thought Yeoman. 'I think I'd like that, sir,' he replied. Hillier put the palms of his hands together and rested his chin on his fingertips, his elbows on the desk.

'Good. Now, you speak some French, don't you?'

'Well, sir, just a bit . . . it's not very good, but I can get by. I managed to make myself understood in France.'

Hillier nodded. 'Good. Well, let me get straight to the point. There's a Polish fighter squadron working up on Hurricanes at Northolt, and they'll be moving here in three days' time. They're mad keen to have a bash at the Jerries, but they've got this bloody awful language problem. However, quite a few of them speak French – it was apparently taught as a secondary language in their schools before the war – and Group thought it would be a good idea if we could find someone who also spoke French to nip across and give them a proper briefing on the organization here. In other words, you've got three days to fly with them and get to know them, so that when they arrive you can help them to fit into the general picture. Do you think you can handle it?'

Yeoman nodded. 'I'll have a good try, sir. I can see Group's point. No matter how good the Poles may be, they probably won't have time to adjust once they get here, so at least some of the adjusting needs to be done beforehand, or the works might get fouled up. It makes sense.'

'Quite. Well, that's about all. The sooner you get over there the better. Take Callender or somebody along with you in the Magister, and he can fly it back.'

Yeoman rose, replacing his cap. Hillier got up too, fishing in one of his tunic pockets. 'There's just one other thing,' he said. 'You'd better put this up. I'm told the Poles are very class-conscious.'

He tossed something across the desk. It was a couple of lengths of thin blue braid, the insignia of a pilot officer. He grinned as Yeoman stared in astonishment.

'Good God,' the young pilot said, forgetting his manners, 'does this mean my commission is through?'

'Very perceptive,' said Hillier. He stuck out his hand. 'Congratulations, but remember one thing. A bit of rank braid doesn't make an officer. I think you are already aware of many of the required qualities, but others you have yet to discover, and some of them may come as a surprise to you.' He reached down and picked a thick volume from the desk, handing it to Yeoman. The pilot looked at it. It was T. E. Lawrence's *Seven Pillars of Wisdom*.

'That book,' Hillier continued, 'was written by a man who, in my opinion, was one of the finest leaders of all time. Oh, he had his critics, who called him all sorts of names after he was dead and denigrated his achievements. But out there across the Jordan, where it all happened, men still talk of 'El Orens' as though he were some kind of god, and it takes a very special leader to leave that kind of legend behind.'

He took the book back from Yeoman and put it down carefully. 'What I want to say to you is simply this. Lawrence's philosophy was simple, and part of it was this; that an officer should never ask his men to do anything he's not prepared to do himself. Remember that, and you won't go far wrong. Now you'd better get cracking.'

Yeoman thanked Hillier for his advice and saluted,

leaving the office in a daze. He went back to the readiness hut and found Jim Callender sitting outside, reading the *Daily Mirror*. He told the American what Hillier had said, and Callender agreed affably to fly his friend to Northolt.

Yeoman had saved the best bit till last, or so he thought. He put his hand in his pocket and drew out the pieces of rank braid, waving them under Callender's nose.

The American got up slowly and Yeoman retreated, expecting to be brought low by a flying tackle. Instead, Callender burst out laughing and produced two identical pieces of braid. 'I was saving this up until later in the hope of being supplied with gallons of beer before I quit the sergeants' mess for ever,' he said, 'but since you're off to Northolt and you're the only guy who's stupid enough to stand me a few rounds I guess the party will have to be delayed a few days.'

He slapped Yeoman on the shoulder. 'Hey,' he roared, 'the erks around here won't know what's hit them! I'm going to dash off and make a list of all the people I want to salute me and call me sir!'

Yeoman laughed. 'Silly sod! Come on, we'd better get ourselves sorted out. If you'll get the Maggie fuelled, I'll go and pack my toothbrush and borrow an officer's hat from somebody. Got to make a good impression on our gallant Allies.'

The flight sergeant looked Yeoman up and down, taking in the hastily sewn-on rank braid and the lighter patches on the sleeves of the pilot's tunic where his NCO's stripes had been a bare two hours earlier.

'Good morning, *sir*,' the flight sergeant said, putting a sarcastic emphasis on the last word. 'You will find Squadron Leader Kendal in operations.'

Yeoman smiled sweetly at him. The man was immaculate, his buttons blinding. 'Why, thank you, Flight Sergeant,' he said. The flight sergeant stared stolidly over his head.

Yeoman took a couple of steps towards the airfield buildings, then paused and turned.

'By the way, Flight Sergeant,' he said, 'your fly is undone.'

The flight sergeant looked down at himself, startled, then turned the colour of a beetroot. Yeoman grinned maliciously and went on his way. He glanced up briefly as a shadow passed over him; the Magister, with Jim Callender at the controls, waggled its wings and blared off towards the south coast.

Squadron Leader Kendal turned out to be a bony man in his thirties, with a nose like a hawk and eyes to match. He was talking into two telephones at the same time when Yeoman entered his office, and swearing fluently. After a while he threw both telephones down and lit a cigarette, disgust on his face.

'Bloody store-bashers,' he snorted. 'Trying to build their empire on clothing returns. Who the hell cares about clothing returns? It's spares we want. Sodding Hurricanes that came out of the ark, guns that jam, bloody radios that don't work. Jesus Christ!'

He bounded to his feet like a jack-in-the-box and ground his cigarette into the threadbare carpet. 'Yeoman! Welcome aboard. Good bunch, these Poles. Undisciplined, though. Chase their own shadows, given half a chance. The only English they know is swear words. Probably get that from me. Don't take any notice of me. Used to be in the Merchant Navy. Bronsky!'

The last word nearly split Yeoman's eardrums. A door burst open and an enormous figure fell into the room, recovered itself and clicked its heels. 'This,' said Kendal, waving a hand, 'is Bronsky. He's the only one of the shower who speaks English.'

Bronsky's face split in an enormous grin and he descended on Yeoman, seizing the pilot's hand and pumping it vigorously. Yeoman backed off, half expecting to be kissed on both cheeks, and took stock of the newcomer.

Bronsky stood well over six feet tall. He had dark, crinkly hair and a face like an amiable gorilla, with bushy eyebrows that met in the middle. Enormous shoulders bulged through his tunic, which sported the RAF pilot's brevet on the left breast and the silver eagle of the Polish Air Force on the right. He wore a flight lieutenant's badges of rank. Yeoman liked him immediately.

'Don't worry if he smells funny,' Kendal grinned. 'They all douse themselves with perfume. Maybe I ought to try it sometime. It seems to pull the women like nobody's business.'

His comments failed to embarrass Bronsky, who rumbled like a volcano. 'Bloody funny,' he said. 'Boss makes same joke every day. One day we nail his pants to bloody flagpole, with him inside.'

'All right, you great ape,' said Kendal. 'Take Yeoman over to the mess and get him some lunch. You can introduce him to the rest of your private army later.' He picked up one of the telephones on his desk and resignedly asked the operator for stores. As they left the office, Yeoman and his companion heard him start swearing again.

There were three fighter squadrons at Northolt, which, lying as it did to the north-west of London, had escaped the pounding that the more southerly RAF airfields had taken. The officers' mess was crowded, and Yeoman, who had not been in one before, felt suddenly strange and uncomfortable until he realized that a great many of the young officers around him must, like himself, be newly commissioned.

They went straight along the corridor to the dining room. It was full, but Bronsky spotted a couple of vacant chairs at one of the tables and steered Yeoman towards it. As they sat down, a tall flying officer with blond, almost white hair looked up from his meal and grinned at them.

'Hi, Bron,' he said. 'Who's this?'

Bronsky introduced them. Yeoman said, 'Good morning,

sir,' and felt immediately embarrassed; the 'sir' had slipped out through force of habit. The flying officer, whose name was Bohanson, took in the ribbon of the DFM under Yeoman's brevet and the patches on his tunic sleeves and smiled.

'New boy, eh?'

Yeoman admitted that he was very new indeed, and they swapped stories across the table between mouthfuls. Yeoman learned that Bohanson was attached to a Canadian fighter squadron, and that he had also fought in France, flying Hurricanes during the final evacuation from the Cherbourg Peninsula. Inevitably, they found that they had some mutual friends. One of them was Simon Wynne-Williams, and Bohanson was distressed to hear about the pilot's severe injuries.

'Still,' he said, thoughtfully chewing a mouthful of apple pie, 'they can work wonders these days. Maybe they'll patch him up all right.' He put down his spoon. 'Well, that's me refuelled. Got to push off now. So long, George. Nice to meet you. See you both in the bar tonight, no doubt.'

He ambled out. Yeoman and Bronsky finished their meal and went into the anteroom, helping themselves to a cup of tea on the way. The leather armchairs were all occupied, so they sat on a broad window-ledge and relaxed in the sunshine.

Yeoman's habitual curiosity got the better of him and he wanted to know something of Bronsky's background. The Pole was forthcoming and told his story simply, with no frills. Later, Yeoman jotted down the salient facts in the notebook he always carried with him. One day, he was determined to write the story of his experiences, and those of his fellow pilots.

Tadeusz Bronsky had been a lieutenant-colonel in the Polish Air Force in September 1939, when Germany attacked his country. He had commanded a squadron of obsolete PZL P.11 fighters, which the Poles called

Jedenastkas. The squadron had gone to its war station on 31 August.

'It was the afternoon of 1 September before we made serious contact with the enemy,' Bronsky said, telling his story in a mixture of English and French. 'We were patrolling Warsaw when we sighted a hundred Heinkels approaching our capital, escorted by Messerschmitt 110s. We only had twenty fighters, but we went for them just the same.'

A shadow crossed the Pole's broad features. 'It was hopeless right from the start,' he continued. 'We shot down three bombers, but the Messerschmitts got eight of our *Jedenastkas*. We lost four more later that day, and the rest of our fighter squadrons fared no better. By the day's end, we had lost fifty per cent of our fighting strength.

'We fought on for two weeks, until we had nothing left to fight with. It was a story of one withdrawal after another, as the Panzers raced across Poland. Our bombers tried to attack them, and were shot down like flies.'

Bronsky paused. Yeoman looked at his face, and was momentarily shocked by the anger and bitterness stamped on it.

'Then came 17 September,' the Pole continued, his voice suddenly low and savage. 'We were patrolling near the airfield of Buczacz with our three surviving fighters when we were attacked without warning by Russian aircraft. The bastards shot down my two wingmen and I had to make a forced landing. A couple of hours later, Russian troops and armour came pouring into Poland from the east.'

'It must have been history's biggest stab in the back,' Yeoman interrupted. He sensed that although Bronsky hated the Germans, it was nothing compared to his hatred of the Russians.

Bronsky nodded. 'After that, there was nothing we could do except get out. I made my way to Buczacz and managed to get on a bomber, one of several which were flying out to Rumania. We kicked our heels there for a few weeks, then the French decided they could use us and we eventually ended up in Paris.'

He set aside his tea cup and smiled wryly. 'Any hopes we entertained of getting into action straight away were soon shattered. The French didn't even have enough aircraft to go round among their own men, let alone a bunch of homeless Poles. There was some talk at one stage of sending us to Finland to fight the Russians, but that scheme fell through when the Finns and Russians signed their armistice in March.

'After that, we got split up and shunted round France from one airfield to another. Some of us, the fighter pilots that is, were attached to defence flights responsible for providing air cover for French towns in the south, and the rest – myself included – were formed into a fighter group equipped with Caudron 714s.'

'Never heard of them,' Yeoman said.

'I'm not surprised,' the other retorted. 'They were bloody awful crates, underpowered and underarmed. Anyway, we got operational just in time to help intercept the big German air raid on Paris on 3 June, and managed to bag a couple of bombers. That was our beginning and our end, really, because soon after that we got orders to pull out to the south of France. Then came the armistice, and we found ourselves on the run again. Like most of my colleagues, I came to England via North Africa and Gibraltar.'

Bronsky looked at his companion, and his face lost some of its seriousness. 'Somehow,' he continued, 'I don't think anyone is going to kick us out this time. It may take a hell of a long time, but between us we are going to win this war. I think, though, that the Germans will not prove to be Poland's real problem. Sooner or later we will have the Russians to contend with, and then our problems will really start.'

Yeoman, vastly interested, was about to press Bronsky

to elaborate on his views when Squadron Leader Kendal appeared in the doorway. He looked around the room, spotted Yeoman and Bronsky, and beckoned.

'Are you fed and watered?' he asked. They nodded. 'All right, I'll give you a lift down to the line. Yeoman, I want you to come up with me and get your hand in with the Hurricane again. Besides, I'd like to see how you shape up.'

Forty minutes later Yeoman, sweating profusely, was hurling his Hurricane round the sky in a determined effort to keep the dogged Kendal off his tail. He had to admit that Kendal was good, very good indeed, which was presumably why he had been given the task of knocking the Polish squadron into shape.

The squadron leader's voice crackled over the radio. 'All right, now it's your turn. Ten more minutes and then we'll go home.'

Yeoman raised a hand and peered into the sun through his fingers. Kendal's Hurricane was sitting there, a dark, indistinct shape poised in the glare half a mile away.

Yeoman smiled to himself and turned in the opposite direction, rocking his wings as though searching for the other aircraft. He glanced back, squinting into the sun's rays, and saw a glitter as Kendal turned after him. The other Hurricane closed rapidly in a shallow dive and Yeoman kept his eyes on it through his rear-view mirror, at the same time continuing to turn slightly this way and that.

Kendal levelled out a few hundred yards astern. Yeoman, timing everything to perfection, suddenly opened the throttle and whipped his fighter round in a tight turn, thin contrails streaming from his wingtips. He kept the stick back in his stomach and the 'g' pushed him down into his seat as the Hurricane wheeled round on its wingtip. Kendal, taken completely by surprise, overshot and Yeoman fastened himself on to the other's tail.

'Tacatacatacatac,' he shouted over the radio, imitating the noise of a machine-gun.

For the next three minutes Kendal tried every trick in the book to shake off his pursuer, with no success at all. Yeoman stuck to him like glue, anticipating every move his superior made. At last Kendal, panting with exertion, called him up over the R/T.

'All right, you cocky young bastard, that's enough for one day. Let's go and meet the Poles.' Still followed by Yeoman, he rolled his Hurricane on to its back and pulled through into a dive, heading back towards Northolt.

They thundered over the airfield wingtip to wingtip, so low that their slipstream furrowed the grass, then pulled up sharply and broke into a tight circuit, curving down to land. As they taxied in, Yeoman saw a knot of figures standing outside the Polish squadron's crew-room, watching them. Even at this distance, Bronsky's huge frame was easily recognizable.

'Not bad,' said Kendal, as they walked away from their aircraft, 'not bad at all. But I wouldn't try those running-away tactics too often, if I were you, or some really determined Hun is going to put lead in your pants. We'll have a talk about tactics later on. We've adopted a few of Jerry's methods, not without some opposition from the brass hats, I might tell you.'

The Poles turned out to be a mixed bunch. Some, like Bronsky, were open and friendly; others cool and un-smiling, formally polite as they were introduced. Almost instinctively, Yeoman picked out the men who could be relied upon in a fight, men who would respond well to orders and the discipline insisted upon by the RAF system.

'Take them up one by one,' Kendal told him quietly, 'and form your own opinions. You can expect them to ask you a lot of questions, since you've been in action much more recently than myself. By the way, there are two more RAF chaps on the squadron, Forbes and Bakewell, but you won't meet them until tomorrow. Forbes is recovering from a sprained ankle and Bakewell has gone to pick up a replacement Hurricane.'

Yeoman flew with three of the Poles before the day was over, and found no fault with the way they handled their aircraft. The best of the three, without doubt, was a sergeant pilot named Sznapka, a diminutive man with a brown, weathered face and fair hair brushed severely back. His first love was flying, and killing Germans came a close second. The other two, Pilot Officers Turek and Sidorowicz, were solid and reliable types who would show up well.

Kendal had been right about one thing. That evening, after dinner, Yeoman found himself hemmed into a corner of the bar by half a dozen Poles, all of them eager to pump him for information on the latest enemy tactics and his personal combat experiences. He managed to make himself adequately understood, his somewhat lame French supported by Bronsky's translations. In turn, he began to pick up a few words of Polish; *samolot*, he learned, was an aircraft, while *lotnik* and *lotnisko* meant airman and airfield. He resolved to improve his vocabulary at every opportunity.

Yeoman noticed that the Poles drank very little, apparently not having much taste for English beer. The exception was Bronsky, who drank several pints in rapid succession before excusing himself and retiring to bed shortly after nine o'clock.

Yeoman was curious about a medal ribbon worn by the big Pole, and asked one of the others about it. He learned that it was the *Virtuti Militari*, the Polish equivalent of the Victoria Cross. Bronsky, it appeared, had been awarded it for ramming an enemy bomber over Warsaw after his ammunition ran out – a detail he had omitted when telling his story.

The young pilot lay awake for a long time that night, considering his new acquaintances. He had never before met a group of men who were so dedicated to the task of killing the enemy, and somehow the knowledge was disturbing. One of the questions they had raised repeatedly concerned the ethics of shooting at an enemy pilot who had baled out, and Yeoman had mixed feelings on the subject. Once, during the Battle of France, he had deliberately killed a German dive-bomber pilot who had been trying to struggle clear of his crippled aircraft, but that had been in the heat of the moment, following a surge of mad fury. Whether he, personally, could do it in cold blood was a different matter.

Yeoman knew of at least two instances where RAF pilots had been shot under their parachutes over southern England, and technically the Germans who shot them had been contravening no rules by doing so. If a pilot baled out over his own territory, he lived to fly and fight again. But to shoot at a German who baled out over England was a different matter, for he was out of the war anyway.

Nevertheless, the ethics of it had to be weighed against one stark fact. The Poles were exiles, their homeland under the jackboot of a ruthless invader, and many of them suffered the daily agony of not knowing the fate of their loved ones. Who could blame them, if their hatred transcended all other considerations?

One thing was certain; the Poles would need careful handling, for their own sakes as well as anyone else's. It would be the greatest test of leadership Yeoman had ever had to face, and if he passed it he knew that he would, indeed, justify the thin stripe on his sleeve.

Suddenly, he felt full of confidence in the future. In the distance, the drum-roll of bombing drifted through the summer night; the Luftwaffe was hitting eastern London again. He smiled, remembering the warmth of Julia's body in his arms as they lay together in the wonder of each other on that first night, and a great peace came over him as he floated into sleep.

Chapter Eight

THE NEXT MORNING GOT OFF TO A BAD START. THIS was the day when the Polish squadron, now fully operational, was to carry out its first combat patrols, and at seven-thirty a section of Hurricanes was scrambled to patrol Rochester at fifteen thousand feet. No enemy aircraft were sighted, however, and the section returned to base half an hour later.

One of the Hurricanes, flown by Flight Sergeant Adamek, developed radio trouble on the way in, and the pilot, already confused, missed his approach and overshot. At five hundred feet his engine suddenly cut out; the Hurricane stalled and heeled over, diving steeply into a clump of trees at the far end of the runway. A brilliant flash and a mushroom of smoke marked Adamek's grave.

The rest of the squadron remained on readiness until eleven o'clock. Yeoman, striving to maintain a relaxed air, noticed the tension mounting steadily among some of the Poles. It affected even Bronsky, who suddenly got up from his deckchair, threw down the magazine he had been reading and wandered over to a dustbin, which he kicked savagely.

The Poles yelled their relief when, at last, the order came to scramble. It was a two-squadron operation in conjunction with the Canadians, who got away first. Yeoman was leading the Polish squadron's 'B' flight, with Sznapka and Turek as his wingmen. The formation climbed hard towards the Thames estuary. The radio was appalling, the controller's voice distorted and intermittent, and the first 'hostile' formation the Poles encountered turned out to be a squadron of Spitfires, sniffing round the sky in the vicinity of Manston.

On Kendal's orders the squadron circled over the Isle of Sheppey, maintaining a steady eighteen thousand feet. Yeoman tried hard to make some sense out of the metallic squawks that came over the radio, but without success. He managed to pick out the word 'bandits', though, which meant that enemy aircraft must be somewhere in the vicinity.

Three Spitfires crossed his nose, from left to right. They went into a graceful, shallow dive over the Thames, the sun dancing on their wings. Yeoman took his eyes away from them and rolled his head to left and right, habitually searching the sky above and behind.

When he looked back, the leading Spitfire was no longer there. It took him a long, dangerous second to grasp what had happened. A mile away, a vivid ball of fire dropped towards the Thames. Yeoman yelled a warning into his microphone, wincing inwardly as the second of the three Spitfires disintegrated in a cloud of smoke and debris.

The next instant, everything fell apart in confusion as a shoal of Messerschmitt 109s came tumbling out of the sky, scattering the British fighters in all directions. The Germans had carried out an almost perfect 'bounce' on their opponents, and for a while it was every man for himself. Yeoman called up his flight, praying they would understand, and turned into the sun, clawing for altitude and expecting to feel the hammer-blow of cannon shells at any moment. Three thousand feet higher up he turned steeply, looking back; Sznapka and Turek were still with him, but there was no sign of any other friendly aircraft. Judging by the excited Polish shouts and curses crackling over the R/T, however, the rest of the squadron were sorting themselves out well.

A pair of 109s passed underneath, rocking their wings uncertainly. Abandoning call-signs, Yeoman radioed his wingmen. 'Sznapka, Turek! *Deux Boches au-dessous! Attaquez!*"

The two Hurricanes fell on the Germans like hawks while Yeoman weaved overhead, keeping a watchful eye on their tails. The German pilots must have been novices; it was all over in less than a minute. One of the 109s exploded on the right bank of the Thames and the other plunged into the river, raising a geyser of water. Jubilantly, the two Poles climbed up to rejoin their leader.

Yeoman's sunward climb had taken his three Hurricanes to the fringe of the main air battle, gaining precious seconds in which to take stock of the situation.

Dogfights were going on all over the sky, spreading inland from the coast as far as Canterbury. Four or five long smoke trails marked the last plunge of crippled fighters. Like an electric light, a warning signal flashed across Yeoman's brain. The Hurricane and Spitfire squadrons were engaging at least four squadrons of Messerschmitts; it was unlikely that the enemy would send over a formation of this size unless the fighters' task was to clear the way for an incoming formation of bombers.

Yeoman turned towards the coast, followed by his two faithful Poles, cursing the inadequate radio contact with Control. The bombers must be somewhere – but where? They could be coming in from any point of the compass between east and south.

Sznapka's excited voice echoed suddenly over the R/T, a babble of Polish out of which Yeoman recognized one of the few English words the Pole had learned: 'Bandits!' Without warning, Sznapka's Hurricane broke away and hurtled towards Deal in a steep dive. After a moment's hesitation, Turek followed suit.

Yeoman went after them, fuming at their lack of discipline. Then his anger was forgotten as he spotted

what Sznapka had been the first to see; a formation of
thirty fat Heinkels, crossing the coast at about ten thousand feet. A few other fighter pilots had sighted them too,
and about a dozen Spitfires and Hurricanes were converging on them. Yeoman put out a hurried call over the
R/T, telling Kendal what was going on, but there was no
response.

Ahead of him, Sznapka and Turek had already selected
a bomber apiece and were worrying them like terriers,
ignoring the return fire that streamed at them from the
others. Yeoman leapfrogged the formation and made a
beam attack on a Heinkel that was slightly lagging behind the others, seeing his bullets knock chunks out of its
starboard wing. He sped over the bomber with feet to
spare and pulled round in a tight turn, opening fire with
his wings almost vertical as the Heinkel floated into his
sights. A large plate detached itself from the bomber's
port engine and its undercarriage leg fell out of its well to
dangle in the slipstream. Dense smoke billowed back,
obscuring Yeoman's vision. Acrid fumes entered the
cockpit and he pulled away sharply, turning to make
another attack.

It was not necessary. The bomber dropped out of
formation and went into a tight spiral, leaving a question
mark of smoke in the sky. Two parachutes broke away
and drifted down.

Yeoman went into a climbing turn and looked around.
The Heinkel formation held its course, but there were
gaps in its ranks now. Two fighters came racing at him
head-on and he tensed, finger on the gun-button, ready
to engage them. A moment later he relaxed; the newcomers were Sznapka and Turek. They dropped into
position alongside him and grinned, giving the thumbs-
up. He shook his fist at them, resolving to tear them off
a strip when they landed. In this case the end had clearly
justified the means, but it wouldn't always work out like
that.

They turned for Northolt, low on fuel, and arrived over the field a few minutes later. The circuit was jammed with fighters, all requesting priority to pancake, and it was a good five minutes before Yeoman and his wing-men managed to slot in. They landed and taxied in carefully to avoid other aircraft which were heading for the dispersals; two pilots had apparently not been careful enough, for a Hurricane and a Spitfire were locked together in a jagged embrace of chewed-up metal, smothered in foam. Yeoman looked for the code letters as he taxied past; the Spit belonged to the Canadian squadron, but the Hurricane was a stranger.

Yeoman shut down his engine and climbed stiffly from the cockpit. His fitter and rigger, Corporal Martin and LAC Turner, looked at him expectantly. 'Any luck, sir?' Martin asked.

Yeoman nodded. 'Got a Heinkel,' he told them, leaving them wreathed in smiles as he walked towards the flight huts. Sznapka and Turek caught up with him and slapped him on the back, chattering excitedly. 'Go away, you pair of bastards,' he growled, trying to keep a stern expression on his face, 'I'll talk to you later.' Sznapka, getting the gist of Yeoman's words, looked suddenly crestfallen.

The Polish squadron's Intelligence officer, Flight Lieutenant le Mesurier – chosen for the post because of his fluent French and smattering of Polish – was having trouble with the pilots who clustered around him, shouting at the tops of their voices and waving their arms. Yeoman didn't envy le Mesurier's job, which was partly to deflate the often exaggerated claims made in the heat of battle. The hardest part was to get the excited pilots to sit still for a couple of minutes while he made some sense out of their combat reports.

Yeoman got a mug of tea and a sandwich from Molly, the plump, matronly woman who ran the NAAFI van and whose smiling face always greeted the return of the pilots, and collapsed into a deckchair with a sigh of relief. A minute later he was joined by Squadron Leader Kendal, his mouth full of pork pie.

'Well, George,' Kendal said through a flurry of crumbs, 'how's it gone?'

'Not bad,' the other replied. 'I got a Heinkel and Sznapka and Turek got one each, as well as a pair of 109s. Had a bit of bother with the buggers, though, not waiting for orders.'

Kendal nodded. 'Yes, we'll have to get 'em all together and lay it on the line. We can't have this privateering. Still, it's been a good effort. We got thirteen confirmed, as far as I can make out, with three probables.' A shadow crossed his face. 'We lost three, though – Forbes, Sidorowicz and Czerwinski. I saw poor old Forbes go full tilt into a Messerschmitt.'

Bronsky ambled across, his face split by a broad grin, with Sznapka and Turek in tow. He nodded at Yeoman and jerked a thumb at his two companions.

'These two want to say sorry for pissing off,' he said, 'and thank you for letting them have their first kills. They say they not go off on their own in future.'

'I'll bet!' said Yeoman, and glared at his wingmen. They looked terribly embarrassed and came to attention, doing their best to click their heels. Since they were wearing flying boots this feat was a near impossibility, and they looked so funny that Yeoman burst out laughing. The two miscreants looked at one another in relief.

The squadron was stood down an hour later. Kendal and Yeoman took advantage of the respite to carry out two practice flights with the Poles, one of which involved an interception on a flight of three Blenheim bombers. Later, the CO of the Blenheim squadron sent a message to Kendal. It read simply: 'Thanks for the affiliation. We're ready for anything, now.'

Kendal showed it to Yeoman, who read it without

98

expression. Poor bastards, he thought, they thought they were ready for anything in France, too, but they still fell in flames.

There was a party of appalling proportions in the mess that night, with the Poles pulling out all the stops to celebrate their first victories as a squadron. It started off fairly quietly, but there was a sure indication of the course events would take when Fred, the steward, scurried out from behind his bar and removed a couple of glass-topped tables to a place of safety.

At one point Yeoman made his way through the beery haze to try and ring Julia, but he learned that she was on VAD duty and returned to the bar, leapfrogging a rugby scrum that was going on in the corridor next to the anteroom.

The bar was a scene of utter chaos. Steve le Mesurier, the Intelligence officer, was seated at the piano, surrounded by a cluster of British and Canadian pilots who were singing 'Balls to Mister Finkelstein' at the tops of their voices. Turek was on his knees at the foot of the bar, trying to set fire to it with a cigarette lighter. He was not having much success, because Kendal, Bohanson and Bakewell, the other RAF pilot attached to the Polish squadron, were busy extinguishing the bar, lighter and Turek with three soda syphons.

Yeoman made unsteadily for the group, dodging a stream of soda water, and tripped over somebody's legs. He fell into the middle of a circle of pilots who were sitting on the floor, pouring beer down their throats at a fast rate. A dripping flight lieutenant seized him by the arm and dragged him into a sitting position. He peered at Yeoman groggily.

'Come'n join ush,' he slurred. 'We're having a li'l comp-comp-comp'tish'n.'

'Oh, aye,' said Yeoman, lapsing into a Yorkshire accent in his intoxicated state. 'What sort of competition?'

'Inna minute,' the other replied, 'one of ush has t'leave the bar, an' the othersh have to guess who it is.'

'Gerroff,' said Yeoman, and stood up. The flight lieutenant tried to grab his legs, missed, and fell on his face. Yeoman staggered up to the bar, picked up a pint of beer that appeared in front of him, spilt most of it down his shirt front, and started quoting poetry to no one in particular.

Bronsky elbowed his way towards him through the throng, steady as a rock. 'Some party, George,' he bellowed. Yeoman felt his knees starting to give way. 'Christ, Bron,' he said, 'I've about had it.'

He looked around him, through the haze of tobacco smoke. Turek was fastening his tie to the rail at the foot of the bar, obviously preparing for a siege, and Kendal was wandering around minus his trousers, shirt tails flapping round his bony legs. His glassy eye fixed on Bronsky and Yeoman and he made a beeline towards them, landing against the bar with a crash and clinging to it for support.

'Wanna find a store-basher,' he said. 'Wanna find a store-basher and punch his bloody nose.'

Bronsky winked at his companion. 'Okay, Boss,' he said. 'There's one in your bedroom. Go beat hell out of him.'

They took Kendal's arms and propelled him towards the door, urging him along the corridor. 'Don' wanna go to bed,' he muttered. 'Bloody store-basher in bedroom.'

'That's okay, Boss,' Bronsky reassured him. 'We'll take care of him. Come on, now, 010 degrees.'

They half carried him up the stairs to his room, dropping him on his bed. He was snoring before they were out of the door.

The party was still in full swing, but both Yeoman and Bronsky had had enough. The Pole went off to bed and Yeoman went out through the main door into the night, pulling his pipe from his tunic pocket and filling it. He lit up and sat on the mess steps, revelling in the cool, gentle breeze that played on his face. From a long way off came the muted drone of engines, and the pencil beams of searchlights played across the southern sky.

Through the open door, the sound of singing drifted to him. Not a ribald song this time, but a haunting Polish folk melody, sung in beautiful, deep-throated harmony by the young men who had made themselves a part of England's war.

Suddenly he was deeply moved, and felt a tear trickle down his face. Half ashamed, he wiped it away, looking round furtively to see if anyone was watching, but he was quite alone.

Then the Canadians started to sing 'Alouette', and the spellbound moment was gone. He knocked out his pipe, rose, and went indoors.

Chapter Nine

'CLOSE ESCORT!' RICHTER SNARLED, HIS FACE WHITE with fury. 'Close escort! The bastards must be crazy! It'll destroy every chance we ever had of getting to grips with the Tommy fighters on more than equal terms. First they switch the attacks away from the RAF airfields, and now this!'

His companion, Lieutenant Schindler, looked around cautiously and took Richter by the arm. 'I know how you feel, Jo,' he said, 'but be careful what you say. If that bastard Kieler hears you, he'll report you.'

Captain Kieler was an administrative officer who had been posted to Fighter Wing 66 a few days earlier. He was known to be a fanatical Nazi, and there were whispers that he was something more than just a Luftwaffe officer. In any case, it didn't pay to take undue risks. Richter and Schindler moved away from the front of the administrative section where they had been standing, and walked past the end of a hangar on to the airfield.

Schindler, a tall, muscular man who had once been an Olympic athlete and was rumoured to have acquired a small harem of French girls since his arrival at Abbeville, grinned at Richter. 'Anyway,' he said, 'it'll be a comforting sight to have you fellows tucked in all around our formations. We've been feeling pretty naked and alone out there, up to now.' He waved a hand in the general direction of the English Channel.

Christian Schindler was a bomber pilot. Despite his relatively low rank, he was the commander of a squadron of Junkers 88 dive-bombers which had flown into Abbeville a week earlier. He was noted as one of the best dive-bomber pilots in the Luftwaffe, but his outspoken views had stifled his chances of promotion several times. Nevertheless, his superiors on the staff of General Kesselring's Air Fleet Two had been shrewd enough to employ his talents to the full, and so he had been appointed to command a special duties dive-bomber unit known as Sondergruppe 320. Originally its task had been to make precision attacks on small but vital targets such as the radar stations along the south coast of England, but now it had become just another bomber squadron taking part in the big Luftwaffe air offensive against London, a fact that disgusted Schindler and his crews. They could, Schindler maintained with justification, have done far more damage by continuing to make surprise attacks on the British radar, or on Fighter Command's vital sector stations.

If Hitler and Goering thought they could break the morale of the British people by sustained air attacks on London, thought Richter, then someone was giving them poor advice. Anyone who had fought the Tommies over France or southern England could tell a different story. These daylight attacks on the British capital were wasting the Luftwaffe's most experienced bomber crews at an appalling rate. For the life of them, the pilots could not understand why the concentrated raids on Fighter Command's airfields had not been allowed to continue. That was the only logical way to bring the RAF to its knees; the present strategy seemed foolhardy. True, London was reeling under the day and night onslaught – but the RAF remained undefeated, and until it was knocked out the promised invasion would be a risky venture.

With the emphasis now switched away from attacks on the British fighter airfields, the only alternative was to bring the Spitfires and Hurricanes to combat and shoot them down in sufficient numbers to achieve the air superiority necessary for the invasion, and this could only be done if the German fighter pilots were permitted a high degree of autonomy. During August, the German fighter squadrons had specialized in what the Luftwaffe termed '*freie jagd*', or free hunting, in which the Messerschmitt Geschwader had swept the English sky in a bid to clear the way for the bombers. The orders that dispensed with *freie jagd*, and instead tied the fighters to close escort, seemed unnecessary and foolhardy. At one stroke, they hamstrung the movements of the German fighter squadrons and handed the initiative to the RAF.

Richter was unhappy. Although many of his friends remained optimistic, he knew in his heart that the Luftwaffe had already lost the Battle of the Island. He saw no hope of an invasion taking place with the September tides, and once September had gone the autumn weather would destroy any further prospect until the spring. As Schindler had remarked pessimistically just a short while earlier: 'This bloody war looks like going on for ever.'

Richter's latest assignment did nothing to improve his good humour. In order to ensure good liaison between the bombers and their escorting fighters, an experienced fighter pilot was to fly operationally with each bomber group, observing developments from the lead aircraft and subsequently making a detailed report to Air Fleet Headquarters, with recommendations on how fighter-bomber affiliation could be bettered – assuming, of course, that he got back to make his report at all.

It was just his luck, the pilot reflected ruefully, that he should be the one selected from Fighter Wing 66 – the penalty for having twenty kills to his credit and an 'above average' rating. The only bright spot was that he had been assigned to fly with Schindler; he had developed a great affection for the bomber pilot in the short time he had known him, and had the utmost respect for his capabilities.

The pair stood in the morning sunshine and surveyed the activity in front of them, as ground crews fuelled and armed the Messerschmitts of Fighter Wing 66 and the adjacent Junkers 88s of Schindler's Sondergruppe 320.

'Well,' Richter remarked, 'I'll soon know what it's like to be on the receiving end. I can't pretend I'm looking forward to it.'

Schindler fished out a cigar from the pocket of his tunic and lit it. 'Don't worry,' he said. 'If the Intelligence reports are correct, we should be able to walk all over the Tommies today. It will be the biggest effort so far. We're putting more than seven hundred bombers into the air, as you heard at the briefing. Intelligence reckon that if we can keep up the pressure throughout the day the RAF will be on its knees by nightfall.'

Richter looked away. He wished he could share his friend's optimism. He looked at his watch: the hands were creeping towards ten o'clock. Take off was in forty-five minutes. The date was Sunday 15 September 1940.

Yeoman walked into the crew-room and hung his Mae West on a peg. 'Hi, Jim,' he said, catching sight of Callender behind a newspaper, 'what's going on? The erks pounced on us as soon as we landed and started refuelling before our feet hit the deck.'

Callender tossed his newspaper aside. 'Another invasion scare,' he said. 'We're going to cockpit readiness in ten minutes.' He grinned. 'Nice to have you back. How's your Polish?'

'Improving gradually,' Yeoman smiled. 'I'm staying with them for another week or so until they learn the ropes. Any panics while I've been away?'

Callender shrugged. 'No more than usual. The Huns have been hitting London pretty hard, but we seem to be coping. McKenna bought it yesterday, by the way. Took a Dornier with him, though.'

Yeoman made no reply. Sudden death was something one learned to live with, and you didn't talk about those who had gone. 'Well,' he said, 'I'd better get back to the Ukraine. It looks as though we might be busy.'

He returned to the Polish squadron's crew-room and sat smoking his pipe on the grass outside. It was good to be back at Tangmere, and the prospect of action exhilarated him. The Poles were standing around in groups, talking amongst themselves in low tones. Something serious must be in the wind for the squadron to be brought to readiness the moment it arrived. Maybe this was the real thing; maybe the invasion was coming, after all. Well, he told himself, we'll give the bastards a run for their money.

A sudden commotion caught his attention. Pilots were erupting from 505 Squadron's readiness hut and racing for their Spitfires. As they strapped themselves in, the Canadian squadron's Spitfires started up with a characteristic crackle of Merlins and began to taxi. Yeoman watched as they turned into wind and began their take-off runs, lifting into the air and heading east at full throttle. A couple of minutes later 505 Squadron's fighters followed them.

A telephone shrilled, and heads turned expectantly towards the Polish squadron's hut. Yeoman suddenly remembered that he had left his lifejacket in 505 Squadron's crew-room and ran off to get it. When he returned, panting, the others were climbing into their Hurricanes. He jumped on to the wing of his aircraft and learned from the rigger that the squadron had been ordered to cockpit readiness. There was nothing to do now but wait.

Richter screwed up his eyes against the glare of the morning sun, which was climbing towards its zenith, and peered at the sky ahead over Schindler's shoulder. It was hot in the Junkers 88's glasshouse cockpit, and Richter felt claustrophobic and uncomfortable. He could, he decided, do without the company of his fellow men in the confines of an aircraft. He turned his head and looked at the navigator, Sergeant Zimmermann, who glanced up briefly from his chart and winked reassuringly. The radio operator and flight engineer had already closed down their positions and taken up station behind the Junkers' rearward-firing machine-guns.

The Thames estuary sprawled ahead of them, twelve thousand feet below the bomber formation. Richter looked around, craning his neck, at the stepped-up echelons of Junkers and Dorniers, strung out across the sky like dark birds of prey. Speedy Messerschmitts flashed over the serried ranks, their wings glinting in the sun.

Richter wished he didn't feel so jittery. It seemed an age since they had taken off from Abbeville and made their rendezvous with the other bombers over the French coast. He envied his colleagues of Fighter Wing 66, and their hawk-like freedom. They were out there now, guarding the flanks, their fifty Messerschmitts forming a silver stairway into the glare of the sun.

Richter glanced at the clock on the instrument panel. It was eleven-fifty. He heard Zimmermann warning Schindler over the intercom that the target was coming up in ten minutes. The bombers were crawling over a layer of broken cumulus cloud, through which landmarks showed up clearly. Looking down through one gap, Richter picked out a large town; that must be Canterbury. He peered up through the cockpit roof, scanning the sky above and behind. So far, there was no sign of any Tommy fighters. It was as though the whole of southern England was asleep. Well, thought Richter grimly, two hundred and fifty bomb loads will soon wake them up.

The British, however, were already wide awake. Ever since they had assembled over their airfields on the other side of the Channel, the bombers had been tracked by the cold, impersonal eyes of the radar. In the control room of Fighter Command's Number Eleven Group at Uxbridge, Air Vice Marshal Keith Park, the Group C-in-C, had been holding his twenty-four squadrons of Spitfires and Hurricanes back until the last possible moment. Now, with the enemy formations in sight of London, he unleashed them.

In Schindler's Junkers 88, the intercom crackled with a sudden warning cry from one of the gunners, Sergeant Heuss. '*Achtung!*' Enemy fighters on the starboard beam, closing!'

Richter saw them an instant later – a line of black dots, growing steadily bigger, sweeping across the sky above the white banks of cloud. They were Spitfires, two squadrons of them, and they hurled themselves beam-on at the enemy bombers. A Spitfire whistled through the German formation, its sleek, green-and-brown lines elongated by its speed, flashes twinkling along the leading edges of its wings. It was followed by another, and another. The Junkers shook to the recoil of its own machine-guns as the gunners raked a fighter that sped past, revealing the graceful, elliptical curve of its wings. Richter, feeling utterly naked, cowered in the cockpit behind Schindler and had a fleeting glimpse of a line of jagged holes appearing in the Spitfire's fuselage, just aft of the roundel. Then it was gone.

Grey fingers of smoke filled the sky. Hazy fumes from the guns drifted through the Junkers' cockpit, making Richter's eyes water. Away to the left a Junkers dropped out of formation, both engines pouring smoke. There was a sudden, blinding flash as a Spitfire, its controls stiffened by the speed, smashed headlong into a second bomber. Two parachutes blossomed out from nowhere and hung there, tiny white splashes against the darker hues of the landscape below. Something – it was impossible to tell whether British or German – fell through the formation in flames, leaving an arrow-straight trail of oily black smoke. Then, suddenly, the Spitfires vanished as rapidly as they had come, heading back to their bases to refuel and rearm.

The bomber pilots closed up the gaps in their ranks

and the formation droned on towards their target, the docks nestling in the big, u-shaped bend of the Thames.

It was twelve-five. In the underground operations centre of Number Eleven Group, Air Vice Marshal Park looked at the status board; his last six fighter squadrons had been ordered to take off and a further five were being sent to his aid by Number Twelve Group, on the northern fringe of the battle.

Park turned to the man by his side, the most important visitor Number Eleven Group had ever entertained, except for King George VI himself. An hour earlier, on an impulse, Prime Minister Winston Churchill, accompanied by his wife, had motored over to Uxbridge from Chequers to watch the course of the battle from its nerve centre. In silence, he followed events from the raised controller's platform, looking down into the big room with its plotting table showing the battle situation. As fresh information came in, the coloured raid plots crept closer to London. On the wall opposite, a large illuminated board showed the battle state of every British fighter squadron: which ones were in reserve, which were airborne, which were in combat.

Churchill, who had been silent until now, turned to Park and asked: 'How many reserves have you left?'

'None,' the Air Vice Marshal replied bluntly. 'They are all engaging the enemy.'

No reserves. All over south-east England, from the Channel coast to London, the sky was filled with whirling dogfights as the RAF's Spitfires and Hurricanes flung themselves on the Luftwaffe formations, breaking through the screens of escorting Messerschmitts time and again. The German fighter pilots, in fact, were having a hard time of it. Tied to the bomber groups by the invisible thread of the 'close escort' order, they were bounced time after time by the Spitfires and Hurricanes, attacking from a higher altitude. The British tactics were simple; they would dive down, make one quick-firing pass at a bomber, then continue the dive until they had gained sufficient speed to climb rapidly and repeat the process. Fighter Command was learning its lesson, and the German pilots, forbidden to go after the fleeing British fighters, watched helplessly as one bomber after another went down in flames.

The first two squadrons to get airborne from Tangmere, 505 and the Canadian unit, hit the first wave of the enemy as the bombers were running in towards their targets. It was some minutes before the Polish squadron, one of Eleven Group's last five reserves, received the order to scramble. The pilots lost no time in ripping their fighters off the ground, climbing hard towards the mêlée that was going on over the harvest fields of Kent. The Poles were thirsting for blood, and this was their biggest chance so far.

Meanwhile, Sondergruppe 320 had begun its run-in over the capital. In the cockpit of the lead aircraft, Schindler chewed imperturbably on an unlit cigar butt, holding the aircraft on a steady course as it rode through the waves of flak that the London defences hurled at it. Behind the pilot, striving to keep his balance on the bucking metal floor, Richter winced as the dirty black tufts erupted all around, some close enough to see the flash and hear the crunch of the explosion. His legs ached, and he wished there was a spare seat.

A great ball of smoke burgeoned up into the clouds from the target area. Zimmermann had left his plotting table and now crouched in the bomb-aimer's position, with nothing between him and England but a few millimetres of perspex. Nevertheless, his voice was absolutely calm as he directed Schindler.

'Left two degrees.'

A shell burst under the Junkers with a wicked bang and the bomber leaped upwards on the shock wave. Schindler corrected her instantly. 'Christ, that was close,' he said. 'You all right, Zimmermann?'

'No problem, apart from discovering that adrenalin is brown,' the navigator replied cheerfully. 'Left another degree. You're flying this bloody thing like a mule.'

A Junkers on the edge of the formation blew up in a great, slow explosion as a shell found its bomb-load. Appalled, Richter watched the debris cascade down towards the city, trailing streamers of fire.

'Steady now,' said Zimmermann, 'hold her at that. Steady . . . steady.'

Richter was drenched in sweat. He felt like screaming at Zimmermann to get on with it. Christ, he thought, these fellows have to go through this hell day after day! Suddenly, he felt very small.

'Bombs gone!'

The Junkers leaped buoyantly as the stick of bombs tumbled from its belly and fell lazily towards the docks. Richter breathed a prayer of relief as the pilot opened the throttles and put down the nose, turning away from the hellish flak and the snarling, harrying packs of fighters. The fighters, Richter thought bitterly, which fat Hermann had said no longer existed.

The bombers droned away and an uncanny silence fell over London, broken only by the long wail of the 'all clear'. As ambulances and rescue workers struggled among the debris, the city's people emerged from cellars, basements and the deep shelter of the Underground and headed for the nearest pub or restaurant to snatch a hasty lunch. High overhead, vapour trails spread out into feathers of white, drifting on the wind.

The Spitfire and Hurricane squadrons which had first engaged the enemy, their guns red-hot, out of fuel, riddled with holes, their pilots exhausted, struggled back to their airfields to be feverishly rearmed and refuelled by the overworked ground crews in readiness for a fresh onslaught. For the retreating bombers, however, there was to be no respite. The reserve squadrons of Eleven and Twelve Groups caught them as they fled for the coast, their formations already dislocated, and clung to them all the way, harrying them without mercy.

The Polish squadron sighted the Germans ten miles west of Folkestone. Kendal brought his Hurricanes round in a wide curve, climbing above the enemy formation and manoeuvring to cut it off. Yeoman, leading Yellow Section, made his habitual search of the sky before diving to the attack; there was no sign of enemy fighters. The Messerschmitts, low on fuel, must already be well out over the Channel on their way home. He ordered Sznapka and Turek to pick their own targets and dived head-on towards the Junkers 88s.

For a split second, Richter thought the Hurricane was going to hit them. Before he had time to draw breath it grew from a tiny dot to a black, menacing shape that filled the windscreen. Then it was gone, zipping a few inches above the cockpit.

There was a loud bang, a flash of flame and an icy blast of air screamed into the aircraft. Hot liquid spurted over Richter's face, blinding him. Panic churned at his stomach and he raised his hands instinctively, covering his eyes. It was a long second before he realized that he had not been hit. He staggered, clutching at the back of Schindler's seat to steady himself. With a sickening surge of horror, he realized that he was drenched in blood. In front of him, Schindler was slumped in his straps, his headless corpse pumping blood over the instrument panel and the remains of the windscreen. Desperately, fighting down his nausea, Richter clawed his way forward and tore at the dead pilot's harness with one hand, grabbing the control column with the other as the Junkers threatened to fall away in a spiral dive. Someone was shouting incoherently in his ear, tugging at Schindler's body. It was Zimmermann, his face white with fear.

Between them they managed to drag the pilot's body clear. Richter hurled himself into the vacant seat, planting his feet firmly in the rudder pedals and grasping the control column with both hands. The Junkers had gone into a gentle, left-handed dive; she came out sluggishly as Richter applied opposite wheel and rudder, bringing her back to level flight once more.

Half a mile astern, Yeoman stood his Hurricane on a wingtip, pulling the fighter round in a tight turn on the 88's tail. The bomber went into a shallow dive to the right, gaining speed, and Yeoman tightened his turn still more, firing as the dark, twin-engined silhouette entered his sight. His bullets danced over the port engine cowling and he saw them punch holes in the fuselage, just behind the rear gun position.

The hammer-blows of gunfire jarred Richter's teeth. A series of staccato bangs shook the aircraft and a chunk of metal whirled away from the port engine cowling, followed by a thin streamer of smoke. Zimmermann reached over and punched the fire-extinguisher button; the smoke trail turned white and then died away. The engine continued to run, although the oil pressure gauge climbed rapidly towards the red danger mark.

The Hurricane flashed overhead and turned in again for a beam attack. Richter turned the control wheel and applied hard right rudder, swinging the bomber round to afford his gunners a good field of fire.

He looked over his shoulder, seeing the fighter come slanting in, tensing in anticipation of the bark of the Junkers' machine-guns. It never came. Instead, the Junkers shook again to the impact of bullets as the Hurricane opened fire, closing in unopposed.

Zimmermann screamed and fell on his knees, clutching his stomach. Blood welled through his fingers. He tried to struggle upright, turning his contorted face towards Richter, then his wide-open eyes lost their light and he collapsed sideways against the pilot. Instinctively, Richter pushed him away and the navigator's body crumpled in a heap beside him.

Yeoman came arrowing down for a third attack, lining

his fighter up carefully. There was no return fire; his last burst must have killed or wounded the enemy gunners. He closed in to fifty yards and jabbed his thumb down savagely on the gun-button, aiming for the starboard engine.

Nothing happened. He pressed the button until his thumb hurt, yelling and swearing with frustration. The Junkers 88 steadied on a south-easterly heading, droning out of the Channel. It was as though the pilot knew that his pursuer was impotent.

Richter, in fact, had already resigned himself to the fact that he was going to die. He felt utterly calm and detached, as though observing himself from the outside. He felt a vague sense of amazement. The shuddering, vibrating bomber, the howl of the slipstream through the remains of the canopy, the blood-spattered floor – all were part of a dream. None of this was happening to him. In a second, his batman's hand would shake him and he would wake up in the warmth of his room.

Then reality sliced at him brutally, like a knife, ripping away the curtain of illusion. Stark terror replaced it, clawing at his guts. Trembling and shivering in a bath of cold sweat, he looked round frantically, searching for the Hurricane.

A dark shadow fell across his face, startling him. The British fighter was sitting a few yards off his starboard wingtip, slightly higher up, in hazy silhouette against the sun. For an instant Richter had a wild, crazy impulse to haul the 88 round in a last, tight turn, obliterating the Hurricane and himself in a final blaze of anger and revenge. Then the mood left him as part of his brain told him not to be a fool; the Tommy could have finished him easily by this time, and the fact that he had not done so must mean that the Hurricane was out of ammunition.

He was going to live. Almost sick with relief, he closed his eyes for a fraction of a second. When he opened them again, the fighter was gone.

114

Richter took a deep breath and looked at his instruments. Both engines were still running, although the port one was overheating badly. Richter had no idea how well a Junkers 88 would fly on one engine, and decided to risk the damaged motor bursting into flames. Every mile of Channel that flashed beneath his wings meant a mile further from England, and if the worst came to the worst and he had to ditch he would at least stand a reasonable chance of being picked up by the German air-sea rescue. He took a firm grip on the control column, his heart leaping into his mouth every time the damaged engine missed a beat, and pointed the Junkers' nose towards the spot where the promontory of Cap Gris Nez lay hidden behind the shallow curtain of haze that hung over the French coast.

Between the Kentish coast and London, the harvest fields were strewn with the burning beacons of crashed aircraft, shattered mounds of aluminium eaten by petrol-fed fires. Here, in a wood, the torn branches concealed the compressed remains of a Spitfire, the pulped body of its pilot still strapped in the bloody cockpit; there, in a huge crater, a few shards of smoking metal were all that remained of a Dornier, which had dived straight in from a height of three miles, the explosion of its bomb-load scattering the chalky soil over several fields.

There was no time, yet, to count the cost. The defenders licked their wounds and toiled feverishly to prepare themselves for the next round, their eyes on the southern sky. Dazed pilots threw themselves full length on the sun-baked ground and slept, the stink of oil and cordite heavy in their nostrils; others crept quietly away, their stomachs knotted with reaction, not wishing their friends to see their bodies quivering with nausea at the thought of having to face the packs of Messerschmitts again, yet knowing that they would fly and fight as often as they had to, each time until the last.

And beneath her pall of smoke London shook herself like an angry old dog and waited, tensing against the expected wail of sirens that would herald a fresh onslaught, as the sun began its long fall towards the western horizon.

A young gunner on the clifftops near Gris Nez stood up abruptly in his emplacement, pointing out over the Channel. 'Look,' he cried, 'there's another one!'

The grizzled sergeant at his elbow took a bite out of a thick slice of sausage. 'All right,' he muttered, peering seawards, 'no need to get excited.'

The returning bombers had been droning in over the coast for the past hour, many of them with signs of battle damage. This one, flying low over the water, seemed to be in real trouble. It was a Junkers 88, and one of its engines was streaming flame. It headed straight for the cliffs half a mile up the coast, pulling up at the last moment and clearing the tops with only a couple of metres to spare.

An instant later, the burning engine blew up and the bomber went into a diving turn, shedding blazing fragments. Incredibly, it righted itself and hung poised for an endless second, tail down, before striking the ground with a concussion that the men in the emplacement felt clearly. The young gunner winced as the wings tore away, as if in slow motion, and bounced across the ground in a trail of fire. The fuselage, like a torpedo, rebounded into the air briefly and vanished behind a line of trees.

A fire tender and ambulance raced off up the road, followed by a detachment of motor-cycle troops. The sergeant spat over the clifftop. 'Christ,' he grunted, 'what's all the hurry?'

Some time later the ambulance returned, travelling at high speed towards Boulogne. The other rescuers came back more slowly, the motor-cycle detachment halting not far from the gun emplacement. Its leader, a corporal, dismounted and came over, removing his goggles and coughing dust from his throat.

'Got anything to drink?' he asked. The young gunner poured him some coffee. 'Bloody awful mess back there,' the corporal said, sipping the hot liquid gratefully. 'Bodies all over the place.'

'Was anyone alive?' the young gunner wanted to know, with a kind of morbid fascination. The corporal nodded. 'Yes, we got the pilot out, but he's in a pretty bad way. The cockpit broke up, and I guess that's what saved him. He's got some burns and both his legs are broken, but I suppose he'll live.'

The man's brow suddenly wrinkled in puzzlement. 'Funny, though,' he murmured, half to himself, 'he kept on muttering about having to report back to his fighter squadron. Now what the hell would a fighter pilot be doing flying a Junkers 88?'

It was three-thirty, and the fighter squadrons of Eleven Group were once more at 'readiness'. The defenders could hardly believe their good fortune. They had been expecting a non-stop onslaught after the first major attack, and yet it was a good two hours since the first wave of enemy bombers had droned away. Now the Spitfires and Hurricanes were once more armed and ready for action.

Yeoman sat on the wing of his Hurricane, munching an apple. The Polish squadron had claimed six victories that morning, for the loss of only one of its own pilots, and the other squadrons of the Tangmere Wing had fared equally well. Jim Callender had bagged two Dorniers, making him the wing's top-scoring pilot with twenty-one victories; the only casualty suffered by 505 Squadron during the morning's operations had been Honeywell, who had collected several splinters of cannon shell in his backside. The wound was more painful than serious, and Honeywell had been the target of much ribald comment before the ambulance carted him off to sick quarters.

'Squadron scramble! Dungeness, Angels eighteen!'

Here we go again, thought Yeoman, tossing aside his apple core and swinging a leg into the cockpit in the familiar drill that was fast becoming more routine than climbing into bed. All around him, Merlins were crackling into life.

The Polish squadron was first off this time, climbing parallel with the coast towards the layer of cloud that had spread over the sky during the early afternoon. They burst through it a few minutes later and emerged into bright sunshine at twelve thousand feet.

Ahead of them, clusters of black dots hung over the coast, creeping apparently slowly towards London. Smaller dots weaved among the bomber formations, leaving short white trails in the summer sky.

Kendal led his squadron flat out for the bombers, ignoring a bunch of Messerschmitts that came diving down to cut them off. He had already spotted a formation of Spitfires flying across the 109s' path; they would keep the enemy fighters busy while the Hurricanes concentrated on the bombers, which were now identified as Dorniers.

Once again, it was a case of every man for himself. Yeoman made for a bomber, only to be frustrated by a Spitfire which shot across his nose. He saw grey trails stream back from the fighter's wings as the pilot opened fire; the Dornier faltered and turned away towards the coast, dragging ribbons of white smoke from both engines.

Yeoman picked another target and closed in fast, opening fire at 250 yards. The bomber's rear gunner was on the ball; Yeoman felt a series of small hammer-blows as a burst of 7·7-millimetre punched holes in his port wing. He fired again, and what looked like a red light suddenly appeared in the gunner's position. Then, as he got closer,

Yeoman realized that he was looking past the enemy gunner into the main cockpit; the red light was a fierce blaze, possibly caused by flares which his gunfire had ignited. He shuddered inwardly, imagining the nightmare inside the Dornier, the crew's blind panic as they tried to beat at the flames with their bare hands. An instant later the flames burst through the thin metal of the fuselage and the bomber started to go down, its framework aft of the cockpit shrouded in smoke.

Yeoman glanced quickly behind to make sure he was in no danger and then watched the Dornier's death plunge. The twin-finned tail broke off and the rest of the aircraft flicked end over end several times in a kind of forward somersault, then fell away in a fast spin. After two or three turns both wings broke away outboard of the engines, and the now-blazing aircraft – or all that was left of it, half a fuselage and the wing roots with the engines attached to them – plummeted straight down. Yeoman lost sight of it as it dropped into the cloud, but it failed to worry him; there was not much doubt about that one.

He looked around him, getting his bearings. London was easy to locate, for a great pillar of smoke rose up through the clouds, marking its position. The Dorniers must be dropping their loads blind in the hope of hitting something worth while. Yeoman felt a deep pang of anxiety as he thought of Julia; he hoped that she was safe in a shelter, but his reason told him that she would be out in the thick of it, helping the injured. He resolved to ring her later and set his mind at rest.

Four Hurricanes passed above him, a couple of thousand feet higher up, heading towards the bomber formation that was wheeling like a flock of rooks over the capital. He climbed to join them, overhauling them gradually and intending to slide into position on the right of the formation. From a distance of a hundred yards he looked across at the nearest aircraft, which was at ten o'clock from him, and tried to make out its squadron code-letters.

The fuselage had a white-edged black cross stamped on it.

The aircraft were Messerschmitt 109s. Yeoman went hot and cold in rapid succession and his hand tensed on the stick, ready to send the Hurricane whirling down and away from the danger. Then, in an instant, the impulse to run vanished. He became deadly calm and detached, his mind working mechanically as he weighed up the situation.

The 109s were holding their course; they had not yet seen him, their pilots doubtless searching the sky above and behind. Yeoman took a deep breath and dropped back a little, below and behind the right-hand aircraft. He took a quick look round, checking his sight and making sure that his guns were set to 'fire'. Then, very gently, he lifted the nose of his fighter a fraction and slammed a three-second burst of bullets into the Messerschmitt's pale blue belly.

The 109 came apart like tissue paper in a great gout of flame. Yeoman applied coarse rudder, firing at the next Messerschmitt as it skidded through his sights. He saw a puff of white smoke erupt from it; the shining arc of its propeller disc suddenly broke up as the blades windmilled. A split second later the cockpit canopy flew off and the 109 dropped away below.

There was no time to see any more. Yeoman shoved the stick hard into his thigh, then back into his stomach as the Hurricane rolled over on her back. He went down vertically, plunging into the clouds several thousand feet below and easing out of his headlong dive while still among the white folds of vapour. He broke out of the base at nine thousand feet and immediately carried out a steep 'S' turn, looking over his shoulder, but there was no sign of pursuit. He expelled his breath in a whistle of relief and set course for Tangmere. He'd had enough for one day.

Yeoman's two kills that afternoon brought the Polish squadron's score during the day's fighting to thirteen enemy aircraft confirmed and four 'probables', one of which was the second 109 Yeoman had attacked. Sergeant Sznapka was missing from the afternoon's sortie, but he turned up later with a broad smile on his face. He had baled out and come down in a tree in the grounds of a stately home, and had experienced a sticky five minutes looking down the barrels of a twelve-bore shotgun brandished by an elderly but very determined lady before he managed to convince her that his accent was Polish, and not German. After that he had been entertained very royally, returning to the airfield full of tea and buttered toast in a chauffeur-driven Rolls. Sznapka, it seemed, was beginning to appreciate the niceties of English life.

It was with a weary sense of achievement that the pilots of Fighter Command collapsed into their beds at the close of that fateful Sunday. There was no doubt that they had given the Luftwaffe a hammering; nevertheless, the battle was far from over. That night, the sirens once again wailed over London, as two hundred bombers dropped their loads into the lurid streets. Darkness, from now on, was to be the defenders' main enemy.

Chapter Ten

YEOMAN RETURNED TO 505 SQUADRON EARLY IN October. The weather was poor and there was little flying. Wing Commander Hillier bagged a lone Junkers 88 off Bexhill on the fourth, then went off on leave.

Yeoman kicked his heels disconsolately around the crew-room. He felt like a stranger in his own home, for Wynne-Williams and most of his comrades of earlier days were gone, either swallowed up by the sky or posted elsewhere to pass on their skills. Even the indomitable Callender had departed, protesting, for Church Fenton in Yorkshire, where an all-American fighter squadron was to be formed as part of the RAF before the end of the month.

When another of the squadron's pilots was posted to a different unit at Church Fenton during the last week in October, Yeoman seized the opportunity to fly him there in the Magister and find out how Callender was getting on. He made nearly the whole trip at less than four hundred feet, lashed by blinding rain and following the Great North Road until he turned right for Tadcaster. Despite the cold and the rain, Yeoman whistled happily to himself as he cruised along; he was flying the 'Maggie' from the front seat, which meant that most of the driving rain missed him and soaked the man in the rear cockpit.

'Can't beat IFR navigation,' he grinned at his dripping passenger as they squelched across Church Fenton's grass towards the flight huts.

'IFR?' the other queried, through chattering teeth.

'I Follow Roads,' Yeoman replied.

'God,' the passenger said, 'is it always like this up here?'

'Only for ten months in the year. Come on, what you need is a good brew.'

They found Callender in one of the huts, sharing the warmth of an iron stove with a small group of pilots. His face lit up when Yeoman walked in.

'George, you old bastard!' he yelled. 'Just the guy I need to cheer me up. Come and meet this bunch of wasters.'

He introduced Yeoman to his companions, three more Americans and another RAF pilot. 'Welcome to the Eagle Squadron,' Callender grinned. Yeoman looked round the room. 'Where are the rest of them?' he said.

'Oh, I forgot to mention it – this *is* the Eagle Squadron, at least for the time being. It'll take us at least a month to get up to strength. We haven't even got any kites – except for that one, that is.' He pointed out of the window at a decrepit-looking Magister, wilting tiredly outside a hangar.

Later, over lunch in the mess, Callender told Yeoman about the Eagle Squadron, and how it had come into being.

'Remember when we were in France? Well, a lot of the guys back home were keen to come over and give us a hand then, just like they did in the last war when they formed the *Escadrille Lafayette*. This time, however, things moved too fast, and the French folded up before anything could be done.

'Anyway, all the applications originally submitted to the French have been turned over to us, and a lot of Americans are being recruited in Canada. Over thirty trained pilots are already on their way out to us, and there'll be more – many more. What we've got so far is a nucleus, and a damn' fine one too. A couple of the guys you just met flew P-40s against the Japs in China last year, so the experience is there. They're desperate to get their hands on Spitfires and have a crack at the Huns.'

Callender lit a cigarette and inhaled, looking sideways at his friend. 'George,' he went on, 'I've a confession to make. There have been times when I've had my doubts about whether we can win this war or not. Everything seemed to be stacked against us. But not any more. We've a dozen nations fighting alongside us, now, and sooner or later we're going to pick up that little bastard in Berlin and wipe the floor with him.'

Yeoman was in a pensive mood as he flew back to Tangmere in weather that was improving steadily, with watery sunshine breaking through the clouds. He had never seen Callender express himself so vehemently before. We are all changing, he reflected; we all went into the cauldron as boys, and those of us who are fortunate enough to float to the surface are emerging as men.

Disjointed thoughts flashed through his mind. What was it Julia had said, when they were on the run before the German Blitzkrieg in France? Sooner or later, America would make this her war too. Well, he had just seen the proof that her words were slowly but surely coming true. What he had witnessed, to be sure, was only a small beginning; but a beginning none the less.

Then something else pounded at the back of his mind; fragments of his father's words, the words of a man who had fought in the carnage of the trenches. War kills and maims more heroes than it makes. He had a sudden, horrific vision of a million dead men, marching mile on mile in grey procession, and a shudder ran through him.

The sun was shining strongly as he landed at Tangmere, but it took much more than its warmth to dispel the black mood that had settled upon him.

It happened on the last day of October: one of the few really cloudless days in the month. A section of the Polish squadron's Hurricanes, led by Tadeusz Bronsky, was scrambled to intercept a small raid that was crossing the coast at 25,000 feet. A few minutes later 505 Squadron's Red Section, led by Yeoman, was also scrambled.

Yeoman and his two wingmen climbed hard, pushing their Spitfires to the limit. Ahead of them, and still much higher up, half a dozen long contrails speared across the sky towards London. As Yeoman watched, three more contrails appeared, intermittently at first, then becoming more solid and defined as Bronsky's Hurricanes closed with the enemy.

Yeoman was puzzled. The enemy aircraft were now visible as Messerschmitt 109s, but the Hurricanes seemed to be having no trouble in overhauling them. A moment later, he saw the reason why. Six objects curved away from the 109s' bellies and fell earthwards. The Messerschmitts had been carrying bombs.

Three of the 109s immediately headed back towards the coast, dropping below contrail height as they put down their noses to gain speed. With little hope of catching them, Yeoman ordered his section to the assistance of the Poles, who were engaging the three remaining Huns.

The latter were fighting back hard, and Yeoman closed in on one which was firing at a twisting Hurricane. He pressed the gun-button and the 109 broke hard right into the fire of Yeoman's number two. It went over on its back and fell into a vertical dive, disappearing against the landscape. The other two broke off the unequal fight abruptly and dived away, pursued by the British fighters. Yeoman got in a long shot at one of them and thought he had hit it, but the Messerschmitt sped on unchecked. Together with its companion, it drew away gradually from its pursuers. The Spitfires and Hurricanes chased their opponents for a few miles out to sea, then gave up. Together, they set course for Tangmere.

Yeoman drew level with Bronsky's wingtip and looked across. The Pole waved, then stuck up two fingers in a gesture of disgust.

Suddenly, Yeoman felt a thrill of alarm as he caught sight of a ribbon of smoke, trailing from the underside of Bronsky's fighter. A split second later, the fierce glow of flames broke out at the root of the smoke trail. Urgently, Yeoman pressed the R/T switch.

'Bron, look out, you're on fire! I repeat, you're on fire!'

'Okay George, thanks, I can handle it. Better keep clear, though, just in case.'

The Pole's voice sounded calm and laconic. Yeoman moved his Spitfire away, putting an extra fifty yards between himself and the burning aircraft.

The smoke became thicker with every passing second. He saw Bronsky reach up and slide back the cockpit canopy. It moved a few inches, then stuck. Smoke billowed up around the pilot, pouring from the cockpit and enveloping the Hurricane's fuselage in a grey shroud. Yeoman found himself shouting out loud, willing the Pole to get the canopy open and bale out.

A blinding orange light filled the sky and the hammer-blow of a shock wave hit Yeoman's Spitfire, almost sending it out of control. He corrected it instinctively, missing his number two's aircraft by a matter of feet.

Bronsky's Hurricane had vanished, torn apart by the explosion of volatile petrol vapour in its tanks. Pilot and machine had become a whirling cauldron of hot gas that froze instantly, rolling across the sky in a white cloud. Widely scattered debris fell earthwards, trailing thin tendrils of smoke and vapour.

So the valiant, great-hearted Bronsky died, the ashes of his body scattered over the Kentish Weald. They mourned his passing briefly that night, the Poles silently toasting his memory and then throwing their glasses into the fireplace. A few RAF newcomers to the mess, who had not known Bronsky, looked on in amazement; but the rest understood, and some, like Yeoman, joined the Poles in their short remembrance.

'War maims and kills more heroes than it makes . . .'

his father's phrase buzzed around Yeoman's mind like an angry wasp as he lay in bed that night. One by one, the men he had known and respected were being claimed by the embattled sky. How many more, he wondered, would have to die before the madmen who had plunged the world into war were finally brought to heel?

Strangely, he felt no fear at the thought that perhaps he, too, was living on borrowed time. The prospect of violent death had worried him once, but in an odd way he had come to accept it as inevitable, and with that acceptance had come a kind of comfort.

He had never been a religious man, and the thoughts that now crowded unbidden into his mind as he lay alone in his darkened room troubled him deeply. Could it be possible, he asked himself, that all the courage, the humanity, the compassion and the comradeship he had witnessed over the past months were really destroyed by death, like the snuffing out of a candle flame? Or did something remain for ever on a plane unseen, vibrant and powerful, like the forces that held the stars on their paths? He envied men who had gone to their deaths with deep faith, men like poor McKenna, who he had once seen sitting in the cockpit of his Spitfire, helmeted head bowed in prayer, while the Roman Catholic chaplain stood beside him on the wing and gave absolution. Well, McKenna was gone now, so presumably he would know the answer – if there was one. Yet there were others, too, who surrounded themselves with an aura of boyish irreverence; men like Jim Callender, who feared neither God nor the Devil, who found utter fulfilment on the knife-edge of action and who would go to their deaths uncomplaining, if need be. Theirs, too, was a kind of faith – a self-assured confidence in their own ability to match their wits against anything and come out on top. Maybe, in the final analysis, it all boiled down to the same thing.

It was a long time before Yeoman slept that night.

Chapter Eleven

IT WAS BITTERLY COLD IN THE HURRICANE'S COCKPIT, and Yeoman huddled deeper into the tenuous warmth of his fur-lined flying jacket. Fifteen thousand feet below, London burned, a sprawling sea of glowing coals in the surrounding darkness. Yeoman looked down, and thought once again of Julia.

It was 15 November. A lot had happened in the last fortnight, beginning with the signal that Flight Lieutenant King, 505 Squadron's adjutant, had handed to Yeoman on the first of the month. 'Report forthwith', the wording had run, 'to Number 1303 (night-fighter) Flight, RAF Manston, for flying duties.' Yeoman had left Tangmere with a mixture of pleasure and regret; 505 Squadron had meant a lot to him, but the challenge that now faced him far outweighed all other considerations.

The German bombers, shielded by the cloak of darkness, were striking hard at England's cities. Only the night before, the centre of Coventry had been virtually wiped out in the Luftwaffe's most devastating and concentrated raid so far, and the enemy had escaped practically unscathed.

The British night-fighter defences were still pitifully weak. A new and powerful twin-engined aircraft, the Bristol Beaufighter – carrying airborne interception radar and a mighty armament of cannon and machine-guns – had just entered squadron service, but it would be some time before it became available in numbers, and meanwhile the RAF was forced to rely on hopelessly inadequate machines such as the Defiant, hastily turned over to the night-fighter role because of its unsuitability in daylight combat, and pure day-fighters like the Spitfire and Hurricane. Admittedly, one or two squadrons were using the fighter version of the Blenheim as night-fighters, but their success rate so far had been almost nil – mainly because the Blenheim was slower than the bombers it was supposed to catch.

Yeoman smiled wryly beneath his oxygen mask. All that stood between the German bombers and London was a flight of four Hurricanes, of which he was now a part, and even the Hurricanes were experimental: Mark IIs fitted with Merlin xx engines and armed with four 20-millimetre cannon instead of eight machine-guns. They formed a powerful enough punch – when they worked. But stoppages were the rule, rather than the exception, and over the past ten days two of Yeoman's fellow pilots had suffered the frustration of getting a fat Heinkel squarely in their sights only to have their guns jam after the first few rounds.

Yeoman brought the Hurricane round in a wide sweep over east London, keeping well clear of the main searchlight concentrations. Being shot down by one's own anti-aircraft defences was a prospect he didn't relish, and that was a risk 1303's pilots ran continually.

A sudden flurry of shellfire caught Yeoman's attention, a twinkling of shell-bursts flickering across the sky to the north. He opened the throttle and climbed, taking the Hurricane up to eighteen thousand feet. Behind him, a thin contrail spun its thread, catching the beams of the moon. He strained his eyes, trying to work out the pattern of the anti-aircraft fire. The flashes seemed to be traversing the sky from north-west to south-east, converging on his own course.

He turned on to a heading of 045 degrees, climbing hard over the Thames. Anti-aircraft fire was coming up thick and fast now, and the black-painted Hurricane rocked as shells burst dangerously close. Searchlights stabbed upwards, probing the night. Far ahead, a silvery midge was caught in one of the beams and other searchlights converged on it, trapping it in a spider's web of light. The midge began to twist and turn, frantically seeking an avenue of escape as shell after shell erupted around it. Then, abruptly, it fell, a glowing coal in the darkness, to be extinguished among the fires of the city below.

Yeoman continued climbing, pushing his vision to the limit in an effort to locate the elusive bombers. They must be all around him, but with the glare from the searchlights it was impossible to see a thing.

Suddenly, the Hurricane buffeted violently, shaken by some unseen agent. Instinctively, Yeoman realized that he had flown through the turbulent slipstream of a large aircraft. It must have passed very close to him. He turned steeply to left and right, searching for the other machine and cursing the searchlights. There was no sign of it. He decided to take a chance and headed for the Thames estuary, hoping that the bomber was on its way home and that he would catch sight of it when London's glare fell behind and his full night vision returned.

A couple of minutes later, out of the corner of his eye, he had a vague impression of something fleeting across the stars. He turned, blinking to clear his eyes, careful not to look directly at the spot; it was much easier to use one's peripheral vision to locate something elusive under conditions like these.

Excitement shot through him like a lance as two vague pinpoints of blue light appeared, a few hundred yards ahead and slightly to the left. He was looking at the exhaust flames of a twin-engined bomber, flying at the same height as himself.

He dropped a couple of hundred feet and closed in, intent on attacking the enemy from underneath. He saw, now, that the raider was dragging twin vapour trails in its wake, and was surprised that he had not seen it sooner. The vapour streamed over his cockpit as he manœuvred into position, lining his Hurricane up carefully. He felt a terrible impulse to tear straight in to the attack, but resisted it; he knew that if he missed with his first burst, he might lose his target for good.

The bomber was recognizable now as a Dornier 17. He stalked it patiently, waiting until the range was down to a hundred yards. Then he opened fire.

It was the first time Yeoman had fired his cannon at a 'live' target, and he was momentarily startled by the dramatic effect as several pounds of white-hot metal punched into the Dornier's belly, the vivid flashes of the exploding shells lighting up the long, slim fuselage with its black crosses. The bomber shuddered violently and went into a steep, right-handed spiral dive. Red streaks lanced at the pursuing Hurricane from one of the enemy's gun positions, but the return fire was a long way wide of the mark.

Yeoman followed the bomber as it went down, the needle of the altimeter unwinding rapidly. He had no difficulty in keeping the Dornier in sight; its fuselage was glowing with some internal fire caused by his first burst.

At four thousand feet the Dornier levelled out and turned towards the coast in a desperate attempt to get away. Yeoman fired again, and saw white flames burst from the bomber's port wing as his shells found a fuel tank. A moment later the Dornier went into a steep dive. It hit the ground in an orange mushroom of fire, scattering glowing debris. Yeoman flew low over the spot, then climbed away towards Manston. He didn't think any of the Dornier's crew had managed to bale out; the rear gunner had kept on firing right up to the moment of impact.

The Dornier was Yeoman's eleventh victory, and the first kill scored by a pilot of 1303 Flight. The young pilot felt no elation. On the contrary, he felt a little sick at the thought of the lives he had just destroyed. He shook his head, pushing the feeling to the back of his mind, but it kept on nagging at him like toothache. God, he thought wearily, this whole bloody business is starting to get me down.

The pilots of 1303 Flight were clustered round a table in the draughty Nissen hut that served as the flight's dispersal point. It was just after eight o'clock in the evening, and Christmas was only a few days away. The cold December wind blew in through the ill-fitting door, and a cylindrical stove in the centre of the room belched smoke intermittently as though in protest at the intrusion.

Number 1303 Flight's commander, Squadron Leader Christopher Payne, surveyed his pilots and felt an inner glow of satisfaction. They were all good men, and had performed well since young Yeoman had brought down the flight's first Hun a month earlier. The score now stood at six enemy aircraft destroyed, and the problems with the Hurricane's 20-millimetre cannon, although not yet completely overcome, were no longer serious. Moreover, the flight had just received three brand-new Hurricane IIs fitted experimentally with long-range tanks, considerably improving their time on patrol.

Payne's small group of pilots looked at him expectantly. Yeoman's eyes betrayed his wariness, a sharp contrast to the nonchalant air of the Dutchman, Piet Doorn, who stood next to him, puffing unconcernedly at his pipe. Payne grinned. He had known Doorn for years; they had both been airline captains, Doorn with KLM and Payne with Imperial Airways.

The squadron leader straightened up. 'All right, down to business.' He turned and indicated the two men who sat nearby; one was a wing commander, the other a balding civilian with piercing eyes which seemed to Yeoman to look right through you.

'This is Wing Commander Rolands,' Payne went on. 'The other gentleman you can call Mr Smith; that's as good as anything.' Mr Smith permitted himself a frosty smile.

Payne motioned towards the civilian. 'I'm going to give Mr Smith the floor first of all,' he said. 'He's going to tell you what this is all about – or some of it, at any rate. If you please, Mr Smith.'

Smith got to his feet and cleared his throat. Yeoman had been expecting a dry, thin voice; but when the man spoke his tones were deep and resonant. He began without any preamble.

'On the night of 14 November, a large force of enemy bombers attacked Coventry. They destroyed almost the whole of the city centre, and they bombed through cloud. Since then, several other targets throughout southern England and the Midlands have been attacked, all of them with considerable accuracy and some of them through cloud.' He paused, and peered at the men over the top of his half-moon glasses. 'Not unnaturally, this new prowess on the part of the enemy has been giving some concern to my department in the Air Ministry.'

Smith gave no indication as to which department he worked for. That information was highly classified. In fact, he was a very senior official in the Department of Scientific Intelligence, although he had a feeling that if he had mentioned the title to the men in front of him, it would have conveyed little or nothing to them. They fought a totally different kind of war from the department's clandestine activities, but the latter were just as vital – sometimes more so – to the nation's survival.

'After a lot of work,' he went on, 'we have begun to come up with some answers. We now know that the enemy are guiding their bombers by radio beam – or, to be more precise, two radio beams, which intersect over the target and give the German crews the signal to drop their bombs. I won't bore you with the scientific details, but the whole idea is very simple and by no means new. Now, to cut a long story short, radio beams can be jammed, but to do that we need to know two things: their frequency, and the location of their transmitters. And that is where Wing Commander Rolands comes in.'

He bowed slightly towards Rolands, who rose and stubbed out the cigarette he had just lit.

'I don't doubt,' the Wing Commander said, 'that some of you have noticed the occasional odd-looking Wellington dropping into Manston recently.' They all had; the Wellingtons were festooned with mysterious radio aerials. They usually landed at dawn and were tucked away on the far side of the airfield, never more than two aircraft at a time, to disappear just as unobtrusively at nightfall.

'These aircraft belong to a special flight which I command,' Rolands went on, 'and its task is to operate in accordance with the requirements of Mr Smith's department. Needless to say, our main preoccupation over the past weeks has been to ferret out as much information as possible concerning the enemy radio beams.'

Rolands turned to a map, pinned to a blackboard behind him, and indicated two points on the French coast, one near the Somme estuary and the other much further south-west, on the Cherbourg Peninsula. 'After a good deal of work,' he continued, 'we have managed to pinpoint the locations of their two main transmitters. The first, up here not far from Abbeville, was bombed last night – we believe with some success. The master station, however, presents the real problem. This transmits the beam the enemy bombers actually follow, and the snag is that the enemy have very cleverly situated it right in the middle of a small town, which makes a full-scale bombing attack out of the question. We thought about trying a pinpoint daylight attack with a couple of Blenheims, but there are two German fighter wings in the area and the Blenheims wouldn't stand a chance, and anyway we can't risk bombs going off target and killing French civilians. We've got quite enough problems with the French, as it is. So we had to think of something else, and I'm afraid you're it. Squadron Leader Payne.'

Payne rose, smiling thinly. 'That just about sums it up,' he said quietly. 'They want us to have a crack at the transmitter, or rather the transmitter building, with our cannon. The people who've looked at the recce photos, which you will see later, have worked out that we can probably do a fair amount of damage.'

'Enough, at any rate, to keep the transmitter off the air for a while, until we come up with a means of jamming it,' Smith interjected. 'You see, we think the Germans don't yet have many of these transmitters, and if you can wreck this one it will be quite some time before they can install more equipment – long enough to enable us to pull something out of the hat, or so we hope.'

'If we succeed,' Payne went on, 'it will be the equivalent of shooting down an awful lot of Huns. I don't want to pretend it will be easy. There's a lot of light flak around the target, not to mention the fighters, and of course we shall have to attack in daylight. But with surprise on our side, we should be able to get away with it. Now, before we get down to more details, are there any questions or comments from anyone?'

There were no questions, and Piet Doorn supplied the only comment. It was unprintable.

The three long-range Hurricanes headed out over the Channel at two thousand feet. They had spent the night at Tangmere, the nearest RAF airfield to their objective, and had taken off with full tanks. Now, with the dawn over on their left, they were following a heading of 200 degrees towards the Cherbourg Peninsula, the grey and angry sea speeding under their wings.

Payne himself was leading the small formation, with Doorn as his number two and Yeoman in number three position. Yeoman looked at the cold, red light that was slowly creeping over the eastern horizon, and shivered. It was a friendless morning, and the sight of the wave crests made his flesh creep. A pilot would not last long in that December sea, despite the fact that the Hurricanes carried one-man rubber dinghies. These were a recent innovation; hitherto, pilots had had to rely solely on their Mae West lifejackets for survival.

For the hundredth time, Yeoman ran over the attack plan in his mind. They had all studied the photographs brought back by low-flying reconnaissance Spitfires – at considerable risk – until the layout of the target was as familiar as the backs of their hands. The transmitter – a spidery circle of tall masts with the building housing its equipment in the middle, like a spider in its web – stood in a small park on the outskirts of Isigny-sur-Mer, which lay on the Bayeux–Carentan road a couple of miles east of the estuary of the river Vire. There were houses all around the park, and poplars on three sides; the only clear approach lane was from the west, which meant that the pilots would have the rising sun in their eyes. There would be no time for a preliminary run over the target; the photographs had revealed 20-millimetre flak emplacements and machine-gun nests all around, and if the element of surprise was lost the attackers would be cut to pieces. They had to get it right first time. There was one consolation: Spitfires of the Tangmere Wing would be providing cover on the way out over the Channel.

The Hurricanes flew on between the sea and a layer of broken cloud several thousand feet above. The dawn was heavy with the threat of snow, and a few flakes had already fallen. Yeoman peered ahead; the enemy coast should be visible at any moment.

There it was – a dark grey line, extending like a wedge into the sea. Payne took the Hurricanes down to a thousand feet and headed straight for the north-east tip of the peninsula. A few boats flashed under their wings. The coastline was clearly visible now, with spray dancing among the black rocks that fringed it.

The Hurricanes turned left a few degrees, following the peninsula's eastern shore. Ahead of them, the coast fell away in a deep indentation, as though the sea had taken a great bite out of it; this was the Vire estuary and its twin. They were right on course.

The Hurricanes hurtled inland over the flat Normandy landscape, with its earthen banks and tall hedgerows. A straight road loomed up in front, with a town over on the right; that must be Carentan. Payne stood his Hurricane on a wingtip and turned east, followed by his wingmen. They fell into line astern and dropped to fifty feet, the roar of their engines hammering at the whitewashed walls of toy houses and bringing the inhabitants tumbling out of doors in panic.

They flashed over a river and were streaking across the western outskirts of Isigny almost before they knew it. Yeoman had a confused impression of blurred rooftops; only the two fighters ahead of him seemed real. But the spidery masts were real enough, looming up in the distance.

Payne was already opening fire, grey trails streaming from his wings and shell cases cascading in his wake. Yeoman saw puffs of smoke dancing round the transmitter building. Then Payne was climbing away, and Piet Doorn was attacking.

Doorn's aircraft leaped upwards as the pilot completed his run. Behind him, Yeoman took a deep breath, corrected his aim with a little left rudder, and pressed the gun-button. The Hurricane shook with the recoil as his shells pumped out, creeping across the ground towards the building. Chunks of masonry and fragments of wood flew into the air and then he was pulling back hard on the stick, leapfrogging the masts which threatened to ensnare him.

Flak started to come up, a few tufts at first and then

whole strings of it as the quadruple 20-millimetre batteries around the transmitter poured shells after the speeding fighters. As though in a nightmare, Yeoman heard Payne's voice over the R/T: 'We're going in again to make sure. You first, Piet, then George. I'll try and take care of the flak.'

Doorn and Yeoman, keeping low, brought their Hurricanes round in a tight circle, levelling out to make a second run. The grey, freezing sky was lurid with strings of glowing shells. Yeoman, a quarter of a mile behind Doorn, saw a trail of fire lance straight through the Dutchman's aircraft. The Hurricane turned over on its back and hit the ground, showering burning debris over a row of houses.

Horrified, Yeoman hunched low in the cockpit and sped over the wreckage, opening fire at extreme range and keeping his thumb pressed on the button until the last moment. A series of hammer-blows told him that he had been hit, but he held his course, resisting the temptation to shut his eyes. Then, mercifully, he was over the masts and climbing hard, away from the meshes of the flak.

He turned, looking back. Payne's Hurricane was circling over the park, trailing smoke. As Yeoman watched it went into a shallow dive. Burning fiercely now, it levelled out a few feet above the ground and ripped through the circle of masts, snapping a couple of them like matchsticks. A fraction of a second later it plunged headlong into the transmitter building and exploded.

Sick at heart, Yeoman headed for the Channel, the flak baying after him. Behind him, a tall column of smoke rose over Isigny.

Yeoman's Hurricane refused to climb above three thousand feet, and the pilot knew he had a problem. A scan of the instrument panel revealed the temperature and pressure gauges climbing off the clock, and fumes were beginning to seep into the cockpit. He turned his oxygen full on and strove to maintain height, putting as much distance as possible between himself and the enemy coast.

Ten miles out to sea, he knew he wasn't going to make it. The overheated engine was juddering alarmingly; it could only be a matter of moments before it seized or burst into flames, or both. It was a time for rapid decision, and Yeoman made it. With his altimeter still showing a hard-earned three thousand feet, he reached up and slid the cockpit hood open. Then, wincing as an icy blast of air plucked at him, he unfastened his seat harness and shoved the stick hard over.

The Hurricane rolled on its back and the pilot fell clear, pulling the D-ring as soon as he left the doomed aircraft. He missed the tail by inches, and a few seconds later the breath was knocked out of him as his parachute opened with a crack.

The cold, churning waters of the Channel rushed up at him and he hit the surface with an impact that stunned him. His parachute canopy collapsed around him and he clawed his way from its folds, banging his release box. The parachute harness fell away and he clung grimly to his dinghy pack with one hand, treading water while he inflated his Mae West. It had to be done by mouth; an exhausting business, for freezing waves crashed over him continually, blinding and choking him.

The buoyancy of his lifejacket brought him some relief and he rested for a moment, coughing up salt water. Then, his teeth chattering with the cold, he pulled the handle of his dinghy's CO_2 bottle, relief coursing through him as the gas hissed into the yellow liferaft.

The dinghy was upside down and it took him a couple of minutes of exhausting effort before he succeeded in righting it. By the time he dragged himself into it he was utterly worn out and frozen to the marrow in his sodden clothing.

After a while he roused himself sufficiently to take stock

of his surroundings, beating himself with his arms in a vain attempt to keep warm. Nausea rose in him as the dinghy was lifted on the crests of waves and then plunged sickeningly into the troughs between them, soaking him each time with a torrent of freezing water. It was broad daylight now, although the overcast had grown thicker and hid the rising sun. A sudden flurry of sleet struck his face. He had never felt so miserable and alone.

He began to lose all sense of time. A numbness crept through his body, accompanied by a leaden tiredness. After a while, he no longer felt cold. He knew that he was dying from exposure, but strangely he didn't care.

The throb of engines jerked him back to consciousness. He blinked, clearing reddened, salt-caked eyes, and tried to locate the source of the sound.

A grey-painted craft, long and rakish, was churning slowly through the waves towards him. It was a German E-boat. Yeoman could see men moving about on deck. The craft hove to fifty yards away. This is it, he thought; this is where it all ends. All the hopes, all the aspirations. And I don't give a damn.

The E-boat's quick-firing cannon opened up with a staccato bark and Yeoman cried out involuntarily, throwing an arm across his face. A stream of glowing coals crackled above his head.

After that, it all happened very quickly. A great noise battered at him, a deafening snarl of engines. A geyser of water erupted close by the E-boat, and a split second later a huge flower of smoke and flame burst into the air. Flaming pieces of wreckage hissed into the sea. The shock-wave of the blast tore at the man in the dinghy.

The twin-engined Hudson patrol bomber turned steeply overhead, arcing through the steadily growing pall of smoke. Yeoman looked up. Two Spitfires were circling; he could just make out their code-letters. They were 505 Squadron aircraft.

'You bastards,' he whispered. 'You beautiful bastards.'

A sea of burning fuel from the shattered E-boat spread out over the water, pushing its tentacles towards the drifting dinghy; but the air-sea rescue launch that came nosing out of the mist to the north was the first to reach it.

*If you have enjoyed this book and would like to
receive details of other Walker Adventure Fiction titles,
please write to:*

*Adventure Fiction Editor
Walker and Company
720 Fifth Avenue
New York, NY 10019*